"I can see I'll have to keep a close eye on you."

He drew her down next to him and continued, "You're an incorrigible flirt."

She turned indignant eyes toward him. "I am not," she denied, trying to keep her voice calm.

He put an arm around her shoulders, drawing her breathtakingly close. "No, I daresay you're not. You don't flirt. You plan every move you make. You're the complete Eve, aren't you? But you're not content with just Adam. You want every man who comes your way to want you."

MIRANDA LEE grew up in New South Wales, Australia. She had a brief career as cellist in an orchestra, and then another as a computer programmer. A move to the country after marriage and the birth of the first of three daughters limited her career opportunities to being a full-time wife and mother. Encouraged by her family, she began writing in 1982. She favors a well-paced what-happens-next kind of story, but says what matters most "is that my books please and entertain my readers, leaving them feeling good and optimistic about love and marriage in our present topsy-turvy world."

Books by Miranda Lee

HARLEQUIN PRESENTS
1362—AFTER THE AFFAIR
1419—AN OBSESSIVE DESIRE
1481—THE RELUCTANT LOVER
1589—SCANDALOUS SEDUCTION

MIRANDA LEE

Asking for Trouble

Harlequin Books

TORONTO • NEW YORK • LONDON
AMSTERDAM • PARIS • SYDNEY • HAMBURG
STOCKHOLM • ATHENS • TOKYO • MILAN
MADRID • WARSAW • BUDAPEST • AUCKLAND

ISBN 0-373-11614-4

ASKING FOR TROUBLE

Copyright © 1991 by Miranda Lee.

CHAPTER ONE

SERINA recognised him the moment he walked into the dining-room, her heart suspending its beat for a split second before jolting back to norm.

Aaron Kingsley...

After all these years.

It had occurred to her that she might run into him some time, now that she had returned to the central coast to live. Gosford was his home town too.

But this wasn't Gosford. This was several miles away, in the restaurant of a motor inn at Toowoon Bay where she'd been working for a few months as a cocktail waitress. Having to face Aaron Kingsley here at work, under conditions where she couldn't escape after a quick hello and goodbye, was, quite frankly, embarrassing.

She tensed as his gaze swept around the room, not far enough luckily to encounter her tucked away behind the bar on his left.

Yet it was ridiculous to feel relief at the delayed recognition, Serina knew. Once he was seated and his lunch order taken it was her job to go over and ask him if he wanted anything to drink from the bar. Even now he was being led over to one of the many empty tables.

Would he recognise her? she wondered, clinging to the hope that he mightn't.

But she wasn't all that confident. She hadn't changed—not in the physical sense—still having the same strikingly tall and very shapely figure she'd had since she was thirteen, the same long honey-blonde hair, the same big baby-blue eyes. And the same distinctively pouting Brigitte Bardot mouth.

Oh, how she hated her mouth! Would have ripped it out of her face if she could have. Yet mouths were the one thing a woman couldn't really change. Her figure she could disguise with clothes, her hair she could cut or dye. Even her eyes could be altered somewhat with make-up. But a mouth?

There was no hope for mouths. And hers had been the bane of her life.

Serina sighed and began to walk around from behind the bar, her heart thudding away with nervous anticipation. Fortunately, Aaron had brought a newspaper with him, had flicked it open and was reading it. With a bit of luck he would hardly even look up when he ordered, would be so engrossed in the news that he *wouldn't* recognise her.

As Serina made her reluctant way forwards, the image of Aaron sitting there in a business suit, perusing the *Sydney Morning Herald* and about to have a businessman's lunch—alone—was so foreign to her memories of him that, for a moment, she forgot any potential embarrassment. She began to wonder where life had taken him since that ghastly night eleven years ago.

Quite far in a material sense, came one obvious answer as her eyes skated over his immaculate grey suit and air of unqualified success. He was certainly still as handsome as ever and didn't look as if he'd lost a single hair of the thick brown thatch that covered his well-shaped head.

But then, he wasn't that old. He would only be...*what*? She herself had turned twenty-eight last month and he'd been five years ahead of her at school.

Which would make him thirty-three by now. No, probably thirty-four. She had been young for her class, only just twelve as she'd entered the hallowed halls of high school, the same year Aaron had been graduating.

She'd had the most dreadful schoolgirl crush on him all that year. Which wasn't unusual. So had most of the other girls. Aaron was captain of the school, captain of the football and cricket teams, captain of the debating team, president of the school council, as well as the athletics champion and the current holder of the Australian Junior Life-Savings title. All this, combined with his gorgeous bronzed body and sexy blue eyes, had made him the target of every female around.

But he'd had eyes only for Naomi, his girlfriend, a stunningly beautiful brunette in the same class. They had been an item since they were sixteen, both obviously mad about each other. Nevertheless, the community had still been shocked by Naomi's falling pregnant in her final year of high school and having to leave. A wedding had been expected to follow shortly after Aaron's graduation but once again the young lovers had surprised everyone by waiting another year before tying the knot.

Aaron had been very high-profile in the media over the next few years, both locally and nationally, winning many highly lucrative life-saving competitions. He was called the Iron Man of the decade, the events he competed in being physically very gruelling, sometimes involving many miles of ocean swimming, board paddling and beach running, similar to triathlons.

Serina had followed his career with avid interest, cutting out any photos and articles about him and keeping them in her bottom drawer—carefully out of her father's sight. But shortly after Serina had left home his name had disappeared from the sporting pages. She had asked her mother about him a year or so ago, but had found out nothing except that he was working in Sydney somewhere.

As what? she wondered again.

One way to find out would be to ask him, the voice of reason replied as she drew alongside his table.

But embarrassment was a greater force than curiosity. And her priority was to remain anonymous.

'Would you like anything to drink from the bar, sir?' she asked softly, hoping he wouldn't really look up.

But his eyes lifted, stared, and very definitely recognised. 'Well, well...if it isn't Serina Marchmont,' he drawled, folding his newspaper shut and placing it on the edge of the table.

When he looked up at her again she could not help staring back. Close up, his face had a strained, almost ravaged look about it, the dark smudges under his eyes giving an impression of dissipated living. Yet, oddly enough, this didn't detract from his appeal. It gave him a broodingly wicked image that was both disturbing and attractive at the same time.

'Don't tell me you don't recognise me!' he exclaimed with a measure of disbelief. 'I haven't changed *that* much. And you haven't at all, I see...'

His incredible blue eyes narrowed as they looked her up and down in a slow, sardonic scrutiny. Serina kept telling herself that in her uniform of plain black skirt, white shirt and black bow-tie, with no make-up and her hair scraped back into a pony-tail, she looked as plain as she could. Yet still she could feel Aaron undressing her with his eyes.

The old familiar anguish contracted in her chest. Why, oh, why couldn't men look at her and not think sex straight away?

The anguish didn't show in her face, however. She'd learnt, over the years, not to react visibly, to seemingly ignore the looks she got, keeping her dismayed and bitter resentment well hidden.

'Aaron?' she said with cool surprise. 'Goodness, I *didn't* recognise you dressed up like that. You look as if you've just stepped out of the Sydney stock exchange.'

His returning laugh had a decided edge to it. 'Right in one. I was there when it opened this morning and was glad to get out. Damned madhouse.'

She tried to hide her shock. Clearly she failed.

'Yes,' he said drily, glancing at the newspaper which was folded on the business pages. 'I don't believe it myself sometimes. Aaron Kingsley—tax accountant and investment adviser. At least, that's what my business card says.'

His eyes lifted to her face again. 'A long way from surfing, isn't it? Well, Serina? You're a sight for sore eyes. But then you always were. Can you sit and talk to me for a while? Tell me what you've been doing with yourself since...' he hesitated, his expression becoming wry '... since we last ran into each other.'

There was no doubt in Serina's mind what had flashed into Aaron's. A vivid picture of what had happened on that ghastly night eleven years ago.

She had been seventeen at the time, a very silly, very immature seventeen. Aaron had been in his early twenties, happily married and a big success.

Serina squirmed as she recalled the humiliating events of that evening. If only her father *hadn't* given in that once and let her go to a school disco, she agonised. If only Aaron hadn't been there, acting as one of the chaperons. If only she hadn't made a spectacle of herself, trying to get him to notice her by dancing right in front of him. Having taken jazz-ballet lessons all her life, she was a very good dancer, but her voluptuous body had a tendency to make any rhythmic movement an exercise in sensuality.

Of course, in her naïveté she hadn't realised that there could be consequences to her stupid actions, that she might attract the unwanted attentions of other males in the room. But a couple of the boys who had been pestering her at school for ages had seen her dancing and this had apparently inflamed their adolescent desires. They had been sneakily drinking beer as well, making them more bold than usual. They had tricked her into a store-room at the back of the hall where one of them had been in the process of trying to assault her when Aaron had burst in and dragged Serina out from under him.

Aaron had matched his verbal abuse of the boys with some well-deserved physical punishment before insisting on driving a tearful and very distressed Serina home. As much as she'd been grateful to him at the time, she would never forget the disgusted look on his face or the feeling that he'd believed she had been partly to blame for the incident.

But worse was yet to come. Her father had demanded to know why she had been driven home early from the disco—he had been going to pick her up himself. Aaron, perhaps sensing a huge parental backlash for Serina, had tried to water down the situation, saying there'd been a little bit of trouble with a couple of the boys bothering Serina and he'd decided to bring her home early.

Nothing Aaron was to say, however, could salvage her in the eyes of her father. Her torn dress hadn't helped, either. He'd ranted and raved, saying he shouldn't have trusted her, that she was trouble with a capital 'T'. Hadn't boys been hanging around her since she'd been thirteen? Some women were born sluts, he'd raged. One only had to look at her to know what sort of girl she was. Finally, he'd declared that girls like her had to be protected from themselves and grounded her totally till after her final exams, a period of six months. She wasn't even allowed to visit her girlfriends' homes.

Aaron had looked appalled by the whole nasty scene and left, shaking his head. Serina had been totally crushed, for she was not as her father had accused. She was rather shy with boys really, her early developing and eye-catching figure causing her more embarrassment than anything else. She hated the way men and boys looked at her and had never courted their attention. The incident with Aaron had been an exception, and quite alien to her normal behaviour.

As far as boyfriends were concerned, she didn't have any, her father having refused to let her go out with boys till she'd left school. The disco had been a one-off privilege, hard fought-for by Serina's mother who privately believed her husband's attitude too strict and old-fashioned. Mrs Marchmont had been a quiet, gentle woman who, on the whole, hadn't been able to stand up to her husband's autocratic and domineering nature.

Looking back, Serina believed that her father's attitude had contributed to her futile crush on Aaron. She'd had to have some outlet for her normal adolescent hormones. Some girls hero-worshipped pop stars. She had had the local surfing champion.

Her heart squeezed tight as she remembered the pain of her teenage years, the feelings of confusion and torment in her dealings with her father. She hadn't been able to understand why he hadn't been like other girls' fathers, why he hadn't seemed to love her, why he'd had to always believe the worst of her.

Her eyes focused back on Aaron and she wondered what *he'd* thought back then, if he had believed her father's low opinion of her. Probably, she conceded unhappily. He had certainly looked disgusted with her that night.

'A lot of water's gone under the bridge since then, hasn't it?' he said, shocking her with the coldly cynical light in his gaze, the harsh tone in his voice. It struck her that he looked like a man incapable of feeling disgust these days, incapable of feeling any real emotion at all.

A shiver ran down Serina's spine.

The Aaron of old had been a warm, up-front personality, exuding openness and light. There was a bleak darkness in this older Aaron that felt disturbingly threatening. She wondered how his wife coped with the change in him. That was . . . if he and Naomi were still married.

Her eyes automatically went to his left hand, where a wide gold band still rested on the third finger. The sight of it gave her the most peculiarly ambivalent feeling. Half relieved, half disappointed.

It was at that precise moment that Serina realised her schoolgirl crush for Aaron Kingsley could quite easily be revived. This time, however, she wasn't about to forget he was a married man, not for a moment. She decided to cut the conversation short.

'Sorry, Aaron, but I can't sit down. I'll get into trouble.'

He glanced around the dining-room and raised a sceptical eyebrow. 'The place is practically empty.'

Which it was by two-fifteen on a Tuesday.

'I'll just stand here and talk till your order comes,' Serina compromised casually enough, though underneath feeling more rattled than she liked to admit. Her eyes kept going to his handsome face, his beautifully haunted eyes, his long elegant fingers fiddling idly with a fork. She had the awful feeling that a telling colour was creeping into her cheeks.

It was an awkward situation, and one which she should have been extricating herself from as quickly as possible instead of standing there like an idiot, staring at him and getting herself all a-fluster. He could only be getting the wrong—or technically right—impression.

Men needed little encouragement in sexual matters. Even married men, she'd found. Funny, though. There had been a time when Aaron would never have even *looked* at a woman other than Naomi. He'd certainly not looked at her that night at the disco.

But, as he'd said, a lot of water had gone under the bridge, and the Aaron sitting at this table was not the same man. Serina had the perturbing suspicion that *this* man would now have few qualms about taking advantage of any interest she might unwittingly betray.

'Suit yourself,' he shrugged. 'So tell me, what are you doing back on the central coast? Your father finally forgiven you for going off to Queensland after your HSC? Don't look so surprised. It was well known around the area that you'd left home and that your father had ordered you never to darken his doorstep again.'

Serina cringed. She hated that about small towns, the way people gossiped and twisted things. Her brothers had told her years afterwards about the stories that had gone around about her at the time. They had been quite horrendous, ranging from her being a drug addict to running off with a married man to being pregnant. The trouble was, throw enough dirt and some always stuck.

The truth was that she had gone north on a working holiday with some classmates after finishing her finals exams. She'd been going to return and go to teaching college in February, but during one of her phone calls home she'd had this awful row with her father. He'd found out that there were a couple of boys in their group—something she and her mother had carefully omitted to tell him—and he'd immediately decided she had to be sleeping with one or both of them, calling her a promiscuous tramp.

For the first time she'd really stood up for herself, argued with him, told him that she was a good girl and that he would eventually drive her away from home with his narrow-minded and hateful accusations. His retaliation for her daring to say this had been to tell her not to bother to come home, then; to stay in Queensland and find herself a job. He had no intention of supporting an ungrateful, immoral daughter.

He'd been as good as his word, too. If it hadn't been for the support of friends she'd made in Queensland she would never have survived. As it was, any chance of a real career had been dashed, and she'd had to take menial jobs that didn't pay much. She'd tried to improve her lot, of course, and had eventually succeeded in getting better-paid jobs, but practically every time some man would ruin things for her, harassing her sexually till she left and moved on, to another job, and sometimes another town.

Life had been very hard for Serina. Very hard. She had missed her mother very much, had missed being part of a family unit. She'd even missed her two older brothers, to whom she wasn't all that close. At least her father had not stopped her mother writing to her, and she treasured their correspondence over those lonely years. But no one had been more surprised than she when a few years ago her mother was allowed to invite her home for Christmas, then every Christmas after that.

Even so, her father never voluntarily spoke to her during these visits. Occasionally, she would catch him looking at her with a pained look on his face, but when she looked back he would jerk his head away. They'd never been really reconciled, a thought which still distressed her.

'Dad died at the beginning of the year,' she told Aaron stiffly. 'So I came home. Unfortunately Mum passed away too…a few months later. A…a stroke,' she finished, swallowing the lump that gathered in her throat every time she thought of her mother. Their time together had been too short. Far too short.

'I see…' Aaron looked sympathetic for a moment, which soothed her dismay that he had no sensitivity left in him at all. 'I'm sorry. I didn't know. But what of you, Serina?' he went on smoothly. 'Surely you must be married by now, a girl like you?'

It was a perfectly reasonable question. But she found herself reacting with automatic annoyance at the 'girl like you' tag. It was a phrase her father had often used in a sneering sense. Other men had used it too, and it rarely meant anything complimentary.

Stereotyping of women over their looks seemed to be a universal problem—not just parental.

Serina always reacted badly to it. When she was younger and more vulnerable she had tried changing her blonde-bombshell appearance, even cutting and dyeing her hair a couple of times. But she had looked dreadful as both a brunette and a redhead. She still did her best not to flaunt her striking figure, but, as a mature person with much more confidence and self-esteem, she now adopted a harder, tougher, more indignant attitude to those who labelled her on sight as a sexpot. The shy, insecure teenager she had once been had gone forever.

'No,' she said curtly, 'I'm not married. Look, I have to get back to the bar, Aaron. There's a customer waiting.' Which there was, thank the lord. 'Have you made up your mind what you want to drink, if anything?'

'A light beer will do.'

'Fine. Be back shortly.'

She had no evidence that he watched her walk all the way back to the bar, except that the hairs on the back of her neck kept prickling and she was hotly aware of the curled ends swinging across her shoulder-blades with the natural sway of her walk.

Once safely behind the counter, she glanced over his way and their eyes clashed immediately. She didn't smile. Neither did he. But within seconds she was reefing her eyes away, an uncomfortable heat definitely flushing her cheeks now. She found it incredible that an almost unreadable, even hard look from Aaron had rendered her so swiftly to such a state of agitation.

Or was it excitement? A *sexual* excitement?

Yes, of course it is, you ninny, Serina told herself bluntly.

Yet this realisation did have its surprising side, for she had never in her life experienced the sort of sexual feelings one read about in books. The closest she had come to it was that night at the disco when she'd been dancing in front of Aaron. But, after those boys had attacked her in the store-room, Serina had become somewhat wary of the opposite sex, particularly ones who were aggressive in their pursuit of her.

And most of them were, expecting to go to bed with her on a first date, becoming obnoxious when she refused. When she'd first been on her own in Queensland she had dated rarely, and only men who looked 'safe'. But she had never fallen in love with any of these safe men. Neither had she wanted to go to bed with any of them.

As the years had gone by, Serina had become more and more depressed over her chances of finding Mr Right, of falling in love, marrying and having children of her own. Her deprivation of her own family unit had made her yearn deeply to secure for herself a warm, loving man with whom she could create her own family.

Which made her very susceptible to Paul. Dear, sweet, likeable Paul, who was good and kind and solid.

She had been twenty-six at the time and very lonely. She had also begun to believe that she would *never* meet the man of her dreams. Paul had loved her to distraction, and she'd tried very hard to love him back, to convince herself he was the right man for her to marry. She'd even gone to bed with him, thinking his loving gentleness could eventually break through this numbed shell that seemed to have grown around her over the years.

But that wasn't to be so. Sex with Paul had been an abysmal failure, with her just lying there, none of her emotions and senses engaged. It hadn't been unpleasant. It had been worse. It had been nothing. In the end she just couldn't take the step of tying herself to him for life.

Serina gave Aaron a surreptitious glance and her stomach flipped over. The certainty formed in her mind that sex with Aaron would never be nothing.

Of course not, whispered a tiny little voice deep inside. Because *he's* the man of your dreams. He's always been the man of your dreams. Didn't you know?

Any joy was quickly replaced by an angry despair. How could he be the man of her dreams? He's married! To even contemplate having *anything* to do with him was asking for trouble. Big trouble.

Hardening her heart, Serina determinedly distracted herself with making the whisky and soda the customer at the bar had ordered.

'Thanks, honey,' the man said as she handed over the drink.

She gave him her working-girl smile, which was bland and uninviting, but he didn't get the hint and started trying to chat her up as she pulled Aaron's beer. Perhaps the glow in her cheeks had given him the wrong idea. She was almost glad to excuse herself to take Aaron his drink, though not glad to have to face the instigator of her inner upheaval.

'Here you are,' she said, and went to hurry off.

'Don't go.' The words sounded casual, but when she stopped and glanced back his eyes definitely weren't. They were holding hers with an intensity that was both alarming and compelling.

'I...'

The intensity faded as a sardonic smile came to his lips. 'Surely you don't want to return to your admirer at the bar? Much as you handled him admirably a moment ago, he might get to be a nuisance. You should have seen the way he looked at you as you came over here. Come on. Sit down and tell me all about yourself,' he suggested, drawing a chair out for her adjacent to him. 'I'm sure you won't get into trouble. And I'll let you know if anyone else comes in.'

Don't sit down, came the panicky warning.

She sat down.

Weak, weak, weak! she berated herself.

'Well? What do you want to know?' she asked, seemingly nonchalant.

His returning gaze held a disturbing resolve. 'Everything.'

'Everything?'

His mouth pulled back into a slow smile. 'Perhaps not everything. I'll settle for where you're living now; whether you have a boyfriend; and, if not, when you get off here so that I can take you out.'

She sucked in a startled breath. 'You don't waste much time, do you?'

His smile became rueful. 'Time waits for no man, Serina. Besides, I'm unlikely to be coming this way again. I'm only up this far on business. I lead a very busy life.'

'I'll bet you do,' she said tartly, unable to stop herself from feeling disappointed. It wasn't a pleasant feeling to have one's god topple off his pedestal. Worse was the leap her heart had made with his declaration of interest. Temptation began to work its wicked way with her. *No man has ever made you feel like this. Just imagine what it would be like if he kissed you, touched you, made love to you . . .*

'Well?' he prompted.

She steeled herself. 'I live at my old home in Gosford. No, I don't have a boyfriend at this point in time, but you won't need to know when I'm getting off here because I'm not going out with you.'

There! She had resisted.

But instead of feeling virtuous she felt ridiculously desolate.

He gave her a long, close look. 'Why not?'

She felt her agitation growing. *Give it to him straight, dear heart, or you're going to get yourself into an awful mess here soon.* 'I don't go out with married men.'

He laughed, and the sound had a harsh, cruel sound to it. 'How moral you sound, Serina. And how stupid of me. I didn't realise you wouldn't know. I'm not married any more.'

Before she could jump to the conclusion that he was divorced he added, 'Naomi died last year after a short battle with cancer.'

Serina was shocked. One didn't associate cancer with young beautiful wives.

But beside the shock was an elation. *Aaron . . . not married. Aaron . . . no longer forbidden. Aaron . . . the man of her dreams . . .*

This last thought again brought her up with a jolt. No, she had to admit it: he was no longer the man of her dreams. He was different, changed. Through his revelation of Naomi's tragic death shone an understanding light on the changes to his personality. Instead of a fast-living philanderer she now saw him as the embittered lonely widower, treating the world with a harsh disdain born of grief and possibly frustration.

But did any of this put a different complexion on his invitation to take her out? Serina didn't think so. What could he possibly want from her except the obvious?

Her own cynicism irritated her for once. Did she have to colour everything because she'd had some bad experiences with men? They weren't *all* sex maniacs. Aaron was probably lonely and needing some company. That didn't mean he expected her to end up in bed with him. It was good sometimes to just have someone to talk to, and people did seem to like reminiscing over their old schooldays.

Not that Serina's schooldays were worth reminiscing over. Apart from her personal problems with her father, she had not been much of a success at school with her very ordinary grades. Her father had held Rupert and Philip up to her as shining examples of what she should aspire to, but she just didn't have her brothers' talents. Of course, her father had always blamed her relative failures on her interest in boys. Which was ironic really. There had only ever been one male who had captured her interest in those early days. And he'd been a man, not a boy.

Which brought her back to the problem at hand. Aaron Kingsley...

'How tragic,' she murmured, but her heartbeat had involuntarily moved up a notch. 'That must have been very hard for you.'

'It was,' he agreed darkly. 'And on Christine.'

'Christine? Oh, yes, your daughter. You didn't have any other children, Aaron?'

'No,' he said brusquely, his eyes grim for a moment. 'Let's not talk about sad things today, Serina,' he went on with a rueful smile. 'Today I've met an old friend and we're going to go out and have a good time together, isn't that right? You can't have any objections now you know I'm not a dastardly womaniser.'

She gave him a startled look and it struck her again quite forcibly that she didn't really know any such thing. For all she knew he might be exactly that. A lot of years had gone by since she'd seen him as the perfect man. *This* Aaron was virtually a stranger with his black humour and haunted eyes. Who knew what had transpired in the intervening years to form the man he was today?

But all these arguments against him were futile, she finally accepted. She was going to go out with him, whether he was good or bad, safe or dangerous.

'I can't go out with you this afternoon,' she explained far too breathlessly. 'I have to go back to Gosford. The family home is up for sale, you see, and the real-estate agent is bringing a man around to see it late this afternoon. Since the buyer's coming all the way from Sydney I don't feel I can put him off. But I'm not working tonight, so you can...' Her voice trailed away as she realised Aaron was staring at her as though she had grown three horns on her head. 'What...what's the matter?'

'This is amazing,' he said, shaking his head. 'You're talking about me. *I'm* the buyer.'

'*You?*'

'Yes, me. At least, I think so. The description of the house I'm supposed to be looking at is very similar to the one I took you home to that night all those years ago. Two-storeyed and colonial, isn't it, with white shutters?'

'Yes!' She was astonished.

'And your estate agent is Central Coast Homes?'

'Yes, it is. Goodness, how incredible!'

'It is, isn't it? Maybe it's fate, determined to throw us together,' he drawled as his mouth curved back into a dark bitter smile.

Her stomach did a complete somersault. *Dangerous*, that smile screamed. Not safe. *Dangerous*!

Serina sat there, her mind whirling as she worried what she was letting herself in for here, going out with Aaron. Honesty demanded she accept he wasn't on the look-out for a steady or serious relationship with her. He seemed too emotionally bruised over his wife's death.

Which brought her mind back to its original conclusion. Aaron was after sex, like most of the men who had ever asked her out. Simple, uncomplicated sex. A one-night stand, most likely. The combination of his possible past conclusions about her moral habits plus her still single status would make him think he was on to a good thing.

Her whole being flinched at this thought, a savage burst of pride making her get to her feet. She didn't need this. She didn't need it at all. She knew what she was. And she was neither promiscuous nor lacking in self-esteem.

'I'm sorry, Aaron,' she said in a cool voice. 'I'll have to take a rain check on that date of ours. I just remembered—my brother Rupert is driving up later to discuss some legal problems with my mother's estate. But by all means come over and look at the house.'

It was fortunate that Aaron's meal arrived at that point because Serina was sure he'd been going to argue with her. His face had darkened with her abrupt change of mind, closely followed by a thinning of his lips that bespoke a strong determination to find some way around this unexpected turn of events. Perhaps he was going to suggest a late supper or something equally tempting. She decided to use the waitress's presence to make good her escape.

'See you later, Aaron,' she said, scooping the chair back into the table. 'I told the real-estate man I'd be home after four-thirty. If you decide not to come then I'll understand. Have a good trip back to Sydney and don't work too hard.' And with that she whirled on her heels and scuttled back to the bar, post-haste.

She half expected Aaron to come over after he'd finished his meal. But he didn't. He did, however, throw her a puzzled look as he stood up and walked from the dining-room, nodding back with cold civility when she acknowledged him.

A shuddering sigh reverberated from her lungs once he was gone, showing just how tensely she had been holding herself over the last half-hour. At least if he came to see the house, she reassured herself, he would have the real-estate man with him. It was the only comforting thought she could get from the afternoon's happenings.

CHAPTER TWO

BUT Aaron came alone, barely ten minutes after Serina had parked her motorbike in the driveway.

She was in the main bedroom upstairs, just coming out of the shower, when she heard a car pull up outside. Dressed only in her undies, she raced over to the window and watched, with eyes widening and heart pounding, as Aaron climbed out of a pale blue BMW and began walking up the path towards the front door.

Damn the man! She should have known he wasn't to be so easily out-manoeuvred.

Heart pounding, Serina scrambled into her white jeans and multi-coloured cotton top with more speed than the road-runner with the coyote after him. Her long blonde hair was tumbled down her back in damp disarray but there wasn't time to do more than run a quick brush through it and push it back off her face. Her feet had to remain bare as the doorbell sent her bolting along the upstairs hall and down the softly carpeted stairs.

She stopped for a second to catch her breath on the small landing before continuing down the last few steps, arranging her face into a suitably composed expression.

The doorbell rang a second time before she opened it. 'You came,' she said, sounding both surprised and casual at the same time. 'But where's the real-estate man?' She glanced over his shoulder with raised eyebrows, giving the impression that she had not realised till that moment he was alone.

He settled watchful blue eyes on her face, bringing an unnerving lurch to the pit of Serina's stomach.

'There's no point in paying a commission if it's not warranted,' he said silkily. 'If I like the house we could come to a private deal.'

A shiver rippled down Serina's spine at the slight emphasis on the word 'private'. But she quickly dismissed her ugly thoughts as the results of an overheated imagination.

Though, to be truthful, she'd had plenty of evidence in the past that men were not at their best when it came to catering for their physical needs. Some would stoop to just about anything to have a woman they wanted. Yet somehow she didn't think Aaron would have to resort to underhand tactics to get a woman into bed.

'Perhaps you *won't* like the house,' she answered in a slightly caustic tone.

He smiled, and once again she felt a jolt of apprehension. There was something not quite nice in that smile. 'I dare say that's possible,' he drawled, 'but I'll never know one way or the other if you keep me standing out here on this doorstep.'

'Oh...' She hated the embarrassed flush that flooded her face. It had been years since she'd been a blusher and she'd done it once today already. It annoyed the dickens out of her.

Taking a steadying breath, she retreated into the foyer and waved him inside. 'As you can see, it's an open-plan house in the main. Lounge and dining-room to your right on entering, the staircase on your left. Oh, and a cupboard under the stairs for storage.'

His eyes swept quickly around the formal rooms, then returned to spend much more time on her, lingering on her damply waving hair, then travelling over her still-heated cheeks before resting finally on her mouth.

Serina stiffened. 'This way to the less formal living areas,' she directed brusquely, and marched through to the back section of the house where an archway led into an enormous kitchen-eating-family area with beamed ceilings and a practical slate-covered floor. But when she spun round she found Aaron had lagged behind to look at the study, which lay on the other side of the staircase—a very private and attractive room with a large airy window overlooking a small fernery.

She moved reluctantly back to stand at his shoulder and peered over it into the room, any agitation fading as her heart turned over. 'That was my mother's sewing-room,' she murmured. 'She spent more time in there than in any other room.'

'It's a lovely room,' Aaron agreed and turned to meet her shimmering eyes. 'You miss her *that* much, Serina?'

'Yes,' she choked out, and spun away before her emotion spilled over into tears.

He followed her this time when she moved into the kitchen. 'The cupboards are made of real wood,' she pointed out in a brisk, tightly contained voice. 'Red cedar.'

'Very nice,' he said non-commitally. And once again looked directly into her eyes.

Serina steadfastly ignored the rocketing in her pulse-rate and moved on to point out the slate floor and the convenience of the laundry coming internally off the living area.

'That's all for downstairs,' she said after she'd shown him the powder-room and the double garage. 'Shall we go upstairs and see the bedrooms?'

'By all means,' he said.

She flashed him a sharp look but there was not a hint in his face of the dry amusement she thought she'd detected in those words. Still, she was very conscious of his walking closely behind her up the stairs, particularly as her jeans pulled skin-tight across her buttocks with each step. It was to be thanked that her top was loose and fell down past her hips.

'You'll notice that the carpet upstairs is of a more delicate colour,' she said, her commentary having the effect of steadying her nerves, 'and that each bedroom is a different colour.'

He looked at the first two without comment while she prattled on. The third brought a wry smile and a question. 'I presume this one is yours?'

Her eyes flicked again around the pink room with its pretty lace bedspread and tizzy curtains. More her mother's taste, actually, than hers. 'Yes,' she agreed.

Aaron stepped into the room and picked up the silver-framed photo that was on the dressing-table. It had been one of those taken by a professional photographer at a restaurant, this particular occasion being Rupert's twenty-first birthday. She knew the photo well. It was a family shot, with them all sitting around the table, smiling, her father looking more approachable than usual; her mother fadedly pretty in pale green; Rupert handsome and confident in a new suit; Philip not quite so confident at a slightly overweight seventeen. And herself, thirteen and wearing a pink taffeta dress that she'd worn first at her own birthday party several months before.

As Aaron kept staring down at it she began to feel uncomfortable, so she stepped forward and looked down, her eyes following his to the bottom corner of the photograph, where she noticed for the first time that her well-rounded breasts and nipples were clearly outlined against the tight bodice of the dress.

She almost gasped when she was immediately consumed with a fierce sexual awareness, for the side of her breast was pressed at this moment against his arm. She stepped back, a shaking hand fluttering to her throat, but not before she felt her nipples swell to an almost painful erectness within the lace confines of her bra.

Aaron glanced back over his shoulder and looked her straight in the eyes. 'How old were you in this photo?' he asked.

'Th . . . thirteen,' she stammered.

'Only thirteen.' He replaced the photograph slowly and turned to give her another penetrating look. 'Did you find it hard, growing up so young?'

She swallowed. 'It . . . it wasn't easy.'

Aaron made a commiseratory sound. 'I think I know what you mean. I matured young. Six-feet-four by the time I was sixteen. Not skinny either. You start acting like a man, wanting like a man, yet you're not a man. I made a lot of mistakes.'

'*You*, Aaron?' She was astonished. Was he talking about his relationship with Naomi, his getting her pregnant so young?

The corner of his mouth lifted in a grimace. 'Me, Serina. Did you think I sailed through life without any problems just because I won public acclaim? Acclaim doesn't always bring happiness. Far from it.'

'Well, you don't have to worry about that now. You no longer have a high-profile image. You can be your own private person.'

The desolate look vanished from his face, replaced by the same hard, coldly determined expression she had noted earlier. It frightened her. Everything about Aaron was frightening her, from his swings of mood to the way her body kept reacting to him. She wasn't sure how to handle either.

'You're so right, Serina,' he ground out. 'So very right.'

The jangling of the phone's ringing was a welcome interruption. 'I won't be long,' Serina excused, and hurried along the hallway into the main bedroom where there was an extension beside the bed. She bent to snatch up the receiver from the bedside table, but when she looked up she was taken aback to find that Aaron had wandered in behind her and was looking at the *en suite* bathroom. She watched him pick up the damp towel that was still on the floor and hang it over the rail, watched him move over and run his hand over her various jars of skin-care products. She turned so that her back was to him just as an impatient voice came down the line.

'Serina? Are you there? Dammit, Serina, answer me!'

Oh, God...Rupert...the very person she was supposed to be seeing later.

'Yes, it's me,' she whispered, carefully not saying his name.

'What's going on?' he demanded tetchily. 'Is there something wrong with the line?'

'I don't think so.'

'Well, speak up, I can't hear you. So what happened with that buyer who came yesterday? Did he make an offer?'

'I'm afraid not. When he found out there was a covenant that prevented the trees in the back yard being ripped out to put in a swimming-pool he was gone like a shot.'

'Damn. Why Mum put that stupid covenant on the place, I don't know! You should have stopped her, Serina. You were the one living with her at the time.'

'I wouldn't have even tried,' she countered. 'Those trees meant the world to Mum. Remember how she used to measure each year's growth at Christmas? They were important to her, Rupert.' Too late she remembered she wouldn't mention his name. Her sigh was resigned.

'Maybe so,' he argued, 'but what would it matter now that she's gone? Sentimental clap-trap, that's what it is.'

'Sentiment is important to some people,' she pointed out caustically. Not to him, though. All he cared about, he and that extravagant wife of his, was living the high life. No babies or solid family values for them.

'Don't give me that rubbish, Serina. You're as tough as an old boot!'

'Do you think so?' she said tartly. 'Look, Rupert, I must go. There's a buyer here now, looking over the place. Who knows? I might have good news when I see you,' she finished, deciding off the cuff she could pretend Rupert was on the way.

'*See* me? You won't be seeing me. One of the reasons I was ringing was to tell you that Philip and I and our respective spouses have booked a cruise over the Christmas holidays. I wanted to warn you so that you could arrange something else for yourself on Christmas Day, knowing what a crazy traditionalist you are.'

His laughter was dry. 'God, I can still see you arriving last Christmas on that pathetic motorbike of yours, all laden with presents and dragging along a Christmas tree. Truly, Serina, I can never understand what you see in all that rubbish. Still, it's a day off and I dare say you won't spend it alone. There must be plenty of men lined up to while away a lazy day with a girl like you!'

Serina felt like crying. Not about Rupert's last dig. She had grown used to the men in her life thinking she was a swinger. But the thought of Christmas alone—this year of all years—dragged at her heart.

'Is that so?' she said stiffly. 'You might be wrong, you know. But don't worry. You go off and enjoy yourself,' she added, unable to hide a certain amount of bitterness.

There was a short sharp silence, followed by an irritable sigh. 'Don't be like that, Sis, I... Oh, to hell with you! I won't be emotionally blackmailed. You live your life and I'll live mine, OK? Goodbye.'

'*Goodbye,*' she punctuated back and slammed down the phone before realising she had just obliterated her planned excuse.

She turned slowly and encountered Aaron wearing a superbly bland face. 'Rupert not coming, I gather,' he asked with dry understatement.

'No,' she ground out.

'Then you can come out with me after all?'

'No,' she snapped, too irritated and upset to bother with politeness any longer.

'Why not?'

'Oh, God,' she muttered darkly. 'Back to that again. Look, Aaron, I tried to let your ego down nicely. But you don't seem to be getting the message. I don't want to go out with you. I'm not in the market for the sort of *date* you're obviously looking for. Believe it or not, I never have been. Now take your elegantly suited body downstairs and back out into your elegantly upholstered car and go back to where you came from, because I don't...' she gulped in some air '... want to...'

There was no going on. A turbulent welling of emotion was gathering in her throat and she needed every ounce of her energy to dampen down the hysterical weeping she was sure was about to take hold of her.

The silence in the room was electric, with Aaron staring at her with such an astounded look that she almost laughed. Poor Aaron, she thought madly. He probably only wanted a bit of physical comfort, a night of make-believe love. But that sort of sex had never been for her. Call it stupidity, call it pride. But her body was not an object to be used without real affection or caring. As much as she was attracted to Aaron, as much as her body was being stirred as it never had been before, she wasn't about to give in to that stirring, not if it meant sacrificing her self-respect in the process.

The moment passed, the moment when she almost fell apart. But, despite her pulling herself back from the edge of the abyss, she left feeling drained and bereft. 'I'm sorry,' she said brokenly. 'There was no need for me to be that rude. But I'm just so sick of men taking one look at me and thinking they're on to a good thing. So, please... do me a favour and just go.'

When he came forward and took her by the shoulders a shudder ran through her.

'Don't,' she managed to get out.

His hands slipped from her flesh but he remained where he was, her dropped eyes encountering a solid wall of male flesh still in front of her. Slowly, she raised her lashes to look up into wryly apologetic eyes. 'I'm sorry too,' he offered. 'You make me feel somewhat ashamed, because you're quite correct. I didn't want to take you out. I wanted to take you to bed. No strings. No involvement. Just sex and no looking back in the morning. And the truth is ... I didn't think you'd mind.'

The blunt confession took her breath away.

'But I can see I was wrong,' he went on disarmingly. 'You're not that type of girl at all. And, quite frankly, I'm relieved. Because I find that a one-night stand will certainly not fit the bill where you're concerned, Serina. I want much more from you than that.'

He took advantage of her bewilderment to draw her into his arms. She went without resistance, more from confusion than a conscious desire to be there. But, once held in his embrace, next to the solid warmth of his chest, all her senses went into a spin. If he kissed her, she thought dazedly, she wasn't sure what she would do. Would all her high principles hold up against the way her blood was racing through her veins?

'I've always wanted you, Serina,' he murmured, stroking her hair and her back. 'Did you know that? When I saw you dancing at the school disco I was shocked by the way I wanted you. I could hardly stand to stay in that hall. I went lightly on those boys later, mainly because they were only doing what I wanted to do but could barely admit to myself. No, don't move!'

He kept her crushed tightly in his arms. 'I realise that's no excuse for what those boys did, but I'm trying to explain why males act so abominably around you, why your father acted so abominably, why *I* have acted abominably today. Have you any idea what a temptress you are, Serina? No, stop squirming and hear me out, then you can have your say. You have a sensuality about you, an unconsciously seductive quality. You make men want you without even trying. But today, Serina . . . today you wanted back. I felt it when you looked at me, and if you deny it then you're lying.'

She shuddered in his arms, virtually admitting the truth of what he was saying.

His sigh was telling. 'I appreciate you don't want to jump into bed with me immediately. You think if you do I won't respect you. Very admirable. But not necessarily true. We're adults, not adolescents, Serina.'

He held her away from him then, looking down at her with a knowingness in his eye. 'Nevertheless, I'll bow to your wishes and we'll get to know each other a bit better first. And *then* we'll jump into bed,' he finished with a devilish grin.

She stared up at his confident smiling face, wondering why she wasn't answering him back, why she wasn't telling him *no*, that's not necessarily how it's going to be! It wasn't a question of getting to know each other a bit better. It was a question of whether or not they fell in love.

'How about we go downstairs and you make me a cup of coffee?' he suggested, turning her smoothly and urging her towards the door. 'We're far too close to that double bed there for comfort. And while we're at it perhaps you'd better tell me about this covenant I overheard you mention to Rupert. I like the house, but my daughter has always wanted a pool.'

CHAPTER THREE

SERINA lay in bed that night, still wide awake well after midnight. Aaron had brought her home at eleven after dinner and a film, given her a chaste peck at the door and a promise to call soon, then departed, whistling as he'd walked back down the path to his car.

What *did* he want of her? she puzzled as she lay there.

For a moment, earlier in the afternoon, when he'd spoken of wanting more from her than a one-night stand, followed by words about their getting to know each other better, she had hoped he might be genuine, that he was looking for a real relationship, starting with friendship, waiting for a deepening of feelings before they went to bed together.

But she could no longer hope for that.

Aaron had made no real effort to 'get to know her better' this evening. Not once had he asked her anything on a personal level about herself; neither had he volunteered any information about himself, his marriage, his daughter or his business. Over dinner he had kept the conversation to food and wine, then at the cinema all he'd talked about were various actors and actresses. She had been left with the feeling that they had been marking time, that Aaron was playing a clever game of waiting till he could pounce again more successfully.

Which brought her right back to her original question. What *did* he want of her?

Simply an affair, she realised. And felt a deep wrenching of her heart.

Why, oh, why, she groaned silently, couldn't reality ever live up to dreams? Why couldn't men see past her sexy face and figure to the real woman underneath?

Paul had been the only man she'd ever met who had loved her for herself.

Serina squeezed her eyes shut. She didn't like thinking about Paul, didn't like remembering the pain in his eyes when she'd eventually called a halt to their relationship. But it had been for the best. She'd only have hurt him more in the end by pretending every-thing was all right when it obviously wasn't. She'd tried to make it easier for him, even leaving her job as the receptionist of the motel he owned and moving on up the coast. For how could she stay on in that town and see Paul's hurt every time he looked at her?

Yes, it had been hard to turn her back on the one man who'd valued Serina the complete woman, not Serina the blonde bombshell.

She didn't have to think too hard to work out which Serina interested Aaron. Though, to be fair, any man who was at odds with the world in general—as Aaron seemed to be—would not be in a receptive state to fall in love anyway. Maybe in a year or so Aaron would be ready for a committed relationship again, one with marriage as the end result. The trouble was Serina couldn't see him waiting that long before trying to seduce her again.

And, to be frank, did she really want him to wait? All night she had been blisteringly conscious of him, especially sitting next to each other in the intimate darkness of the cinema. She'd found it impossible to concentrate on the film. She'd kept listening to his breathing and savouring the tangy scent of his after-shave. Her mind had kept imagining what it would be like when he kissed her goodnight. By the time he'd brought her home she'd wanted him to kiss her quite badly, wanted to feel his lips on hers, his arms around her body.

But he'd merely brushed his lips against her cheek and left her with a frustration she'd never felt before. Had that been a deliberate ploy? she worried. A clever manoeuvre by an experienced seducer? He'd claimed he knew she wanted him. Was he bargaining that by next time she'd be less likely to resist?

She nearly jumped out of her skin when the phone rang. Leaning over the rumpled pillows, she nervously picked up the receiver, knowing before she heard his very attractive male drawl who it was.

'Serina?'

'Yes...' A quiver ran up and down her spine.

'I've just got back to Sydney.'

'How do you know I wasn't asleep?' She tried to put a reproachful sound in her voice but failed dismally.

'If you feel the way I do,' he murmured throatily, 'you won't have been sleeping.'

The low moan escaped her lips before she could snatch it back. 'God, don't do that,' he groaned back.

She stayed breathlessly silent, but her hand was shaking.

'I'll drive up tomorrow after work,' he rasped.

'No! No, I...I work tomorrow night.'

'Not *all* night,' he growled.

'You're rushing me again, Aaron,' she blurted out in a panic.

He sighed. 'Very well. What night *don't* you work this week? No strings. Just a date.'

'I'm not off any night till next Sunday,' she stated firmly, determined to get a grip on the situation.

'Sunday,' he repeated. 'I have to go to my sister's on Sunday night. Family dinner. She lives up your way, actually.' He was silent for a few seconds. 'Look, why don't you come along too? That should satisfy your sense of propriety. I can't very well ravish you on the dining table, can I? At least,' he added with dry amusement, 'not Jillian's dining table.'

The man was incorrigibly wicked, Serina decided, but couldn't help the madly erotic image his words evoked. A dining table...lord help her, but she found the idea unbearably exciting.

But Aaron's invitation to take her to a family dinner put a welcome dent in her worries about him. In fact, she was thrilled. No man took a girl home to meet the family unless he was on the up and up. Clearly, she'd been too mistrusting of him. Her heart soared with pleasure and relief.

'All right,' she said, trying to hide her elation that he *did* want a real relationship with her.

'Great. Shall we say seven o'clock Sunday evening?'

'Fine.'

'Be ready,' he advised darkly. 'I can't stand people who aren't ready on time.'

'I'll be ready,' she reassured him. With bells on!

'Aaron!' she called before he could ring off.

'Yes?'

'What about the house? Have you made up your mind about it yet?'

'No. I'll talk it over with Christine when I see her on Sunday night.'

'But...don't you live together?'

'Not at the moment. She goes to boarding-school and spends her holidays with my sister. I sold my house, you see, and I'm living in a small unit in the city by myself till I buy a place up on the central coast. I want Christine to do her Higher School Certificate at a local school, where she can make friends for life. I never was keen on the boarding-school idea but Naomi insisted, and after she died I didn't like to disturb Christine's schooling till an appropriate time. She's just done her School Certificate, and a lot of students change schools at this point.'

Serina was astonished by the harsh edge in Aaron's voice as he spoke of his wife's decision to send Christine to boarding-school. For the first time the thought struck that their 'perfect' marriage might not have been all that perfect. She didn't know whether to feel pleased or worried. A bad marriage often put people off the institution for life.

'Perhaps this house is too big for you?' she inserted casually, trying to see if he would confess to wanting to remarry one day.

'No, I like plenty of room and I would always want Christine to be able to bring lots of friends home.'

'I see . . .' No admission there.

'You seem anxious to sell, Serina. Do you need the money?'

'Rupert and Philip say they do,' she said drily.

For her part she was probably the poorest of the lot, with few savings. She had hoped her brothers would let her live in the house for a while. Not so. They were pressing for a quick sale before the market dropped further.

'If you ever need any money or anything you only have to ask,' Aaron offered softly.

Serina stiffened. To accept money from a man meant only one thing to her. 'I'm fine, Aaron,' she said tautly. 'I'm also tired.'

He sighed again. 'I get the hint. Sleep well, and I'll see you Sunday night.'

Six thirty-five Sunday evening found Serina looking in the bathroom mirror, dithering with her make-up. How much she would wear was the problem. She wasn't about to go to Aaron's sister's for dinner looking any less than the mature, sophisticated woman she was, and with her face scrubbed clean she looked about nineteen. But on the other hand she didn't want to overdo things. Fully made-up, she'd always attracted too much attention of the wrong kind.

'So, my dear,' she pronounced aloud to her reflection. 'Just a touch of blue eye-shadow, some mascara, and only the palest of pale coral lipstick. Nothing seductive or sexy or provocative!'

Once done, she stepped back from the vanity unit and gave herself a final appraisal, her frown showing a lingering doubt. The make-up was fine, she thought. But she'd hoped that, by putting her hair up and wearing her mother's cornflower-blue suit and pearls, she would achieve the right understated effect.

But the outfit looked different on her to the way it had on her mother. Much more...alluring, the knitted material clinging to her more generous curves. Not that it was a provocative garment, the style being quite plain, the top round-necked and short-sleeved, the skirt following the line of her hips before swirling out from knee to mid-calf.

Serina puffed the top into a more blouson effect, trying to lessen the impact of her unfortunately memorable bust. But this didn't work, making the skirt look too long. With a resigned sigh she eased the top back down to where it gave the right balance.

As the digital bedside clock clicked over to six fifty-two Serina resigned herself to her appearance—at least her hair looked subdued and elegant—picked up her mother's white Oroton evening-bag, slipped her stockinged feet into the dainty blue sandals that matched the outfit and hurried downstairs, where her coral nail-polish awaited on the kitchen table. She was just finishing the last nail when the doorbell rang.

Her heart jumped with surprise, but a quick look at her slim gold watch confirmed it was exactly seven o'clock. She raised her eyebrows, not used to people's being so punctual. But then Aaron had been vehement about her being ready.

Easing the nail-brush back into the bottle, Serina rose and walked slowly towards the front door, her hands flapping in an effort to instant-dry her nails. Her heart was flapping as well, and she dragged in several steadying breaths as she approached the front door.

One unsuccessful try at turning the smooth brass knob with the palm of her hand had her bristling with self-irritation. On the third attempt she gave up. By this time he had rung the bell again.

'I've just painted my nails, Aaron,' she called out, 'and I can't open the door. Just come in. It's not locked.'

The door opened inwards so abruptly that Serina had to skip quickly backwards or be sent flying. 'Sorry,' he muttered, and turned to close the door behind him, giving Serina the opportunity for a brief, though unobserved scrutiny of his appearance.

Not quite so much the formidable business executive tonight, she noticed with a measure of relief, the casual fawn trousers, open-necked black shirt and zippered cream jacket reminding her more of the

Aaron of old. But he was still breathtakingly handsome and sexy. Already she could feel her heart-rate pick up, and with it her worry level. Did he realise how vulnerable she was to him? She hoped not. She really wanted them to become much better acquainted before their relationship was complicated by sex. How would she ever be sure of him otherwise?

She was gathering herself to give him a suitably composed smile of greeting when he wheeled back to face her, a disapproving look on his face.

'You know, Serina,' he growled, 'you really should lock your doors at all times. The statistics on house burglary are simply frightening. Not to mention rape...' His voice trailed away, his blue eyes glittering disturbingly as they raked over her figure.

She stopped flapping her hands, her mouth going uncomfortably dry, her stomach somersaulting. But then she realised how important it was to act normally and not dissolve into wimpish mush every time he looked at her.

So she lifted confident eyes and drummed up a wry smile. 'And good evening to you, too, Mr Kingsley. Might I ask if your concern is for me and mine, or for what might shortly be yours?' Too late she realised that that could be taken the wrong way. But she decided to brazen it out, and raised a sassy-looking eyebrow at him.

For a few lengthy seconds his frown remained, but then a slow smile took over. It was lop-sided and engaging, bringing a seductive warmth to his gorgeous blue eyes.

Serina gulped.

'Telling me to mind my own business, are you?' he chuckled.

She tried to ignore her pulse-beat, which was doing a tango all on its own. 'Men have this awful failing,' she countered, 'for dishing out advice to women, even when not asked. Some women don't like it.'

He slanted her a dry, though amused look. 'Is that so? I'll try to remember that, Miss Independent. Or is it Ms?'

She started blowing on her nails. It was a good excuse for dropping her eyes from his. 'Oh, definitely not Ms. Sounds like a bee caught in a bottle.'

Aaron laughed, and for the first time since she'd met him again he sounded happy. Serina felt a flush of self-satisfaction. See, Aaron Kingsley, she wanted to say. I'm good company out of bed too. And I aim to make you realise that.

'Those nails dry yet?' he asked, still smiling. 'Dinner won't wait indefinitely. Or, should I say, Jillian won't. You know older sisters. Mother hens, all of them.'

'Oh? So it's your sister who's the stickler for punctuality, is it?' Serina grinned. 'I was wondering who it was that had turned you into a clock-watcher.'

The change in Aaron was immediate and almost alarming. His face tightened, his eyes darkening with annoyance. 'We all have our faults,' he snapped.

Serina was taken aback. 'I . . . I'll just get the house keys and my bag and we can be going,' she said, whirling away, her skirt swirling around her legs as she hurried, frowning, to where she had left her things on the kitchen counter.

She puzzled over Aaron's reaction till she put it down to work-stress. The world, she believed, had sped up to a frenetic pace over the past decade, and most people countered the stress by consciously relaxing in their leisure time, and being somewhat less hung up on old values like strict punctuality. In fact, most of the time, people didn't pin others down to a definite arrival or departure time. She decided Aaron needed someone to show him that the world wouldn't come to an end if he was a few minutes late occasionally.

She was thinking about that as she walked back to her handsome but uptight escort, who had stayed where he was, near the front door. But any mulling over of his possible stress problems was distracted when she noticed how avidly he was watching the movements of her figure as she approached.

'How lovely you are, Serina,' he murmured, any earlier irritation with her obviously forgotten.

She wanted to lick dry lips but dared not. 'Thank you,' she said hoarsely.

'But I prefer your hair down. I'll take it down later.'

Serina's heart leapt. Just in time she composed herself, her glance becoming cold and reproachful.

'Might I remind you, Aaron,' she said with a frostiness she had perfected on other men over the years, 'that you said tonight was just a date? No strings.'

He returned her look, chill for chill. Once again she felt a quiver of alarm at the hard resolve his eyes could project so quickly. Was this the look of a man who *cared* about her?

'Did I?' he drawled.

'Yes,' she said, shaken.

A smile followed, but it was not a smile of real warmth. 'I dare say I can be patient a little longer. It's up to you.' He took her elbow and ushered her from the house.

Somehow Serina didn't find much relief in Aaron's smoothly delivered reassurance. Or that last tacked-on remark. Did he mean he would still try to seduce her later? She had an awful feeling he would, hoping she would give in and let him make love to her. The awful truth was that it was a distinct possibility. But the arrogance of his presumption fired a bitter resolve not to capitulate.

Patience, she thought crossly as she locked up the front door. Men like Aaron had never really learnt patience. Everything came to them too quickly, too easily. Love, women, success ... The world was their oyster.

But then she remembered his wife's death and felt guilt-ridden. He certainly hadn't had it easy lately. Not by a long shot. This realisation didn't change her resolve not to let Aaron make love to her tonight, but it did make her determine not to be bitchy about it. And to try to make their evening together still as pleasurable as possible.

Slipping the keys in her bag, she smiled up at him. 'All safe and sound! Now, tell me about your sister, Aaron, so I won't be ignorant when I arrive. You said she was older. How much older?'

'Almost twenty years, actually. She's my only family left now, and she rather fancies herself my mother rather than my sister. Which reminds me, I must warn you that you'll come as a bit of a shock to her.'

Serina was taken aback. 'A shock? Why should I be a shock?'

Aaron's eyes took on an amused light. 'Ever since I became a widower, Jillian's been trying to match-make me with every available divorcee and widow she can find. All in their late thirties and very matronly, to say the least. She thinks it's her duty to see me happily settled. And to her, being happily settled for a man means a wife who can clean and cook and keep house. Unfortunately, she and I differ about what will make me happy...'

His smile was definitely full of meaning as he looked down at her and, although she should have been almost offended that he thought her forte was far removed from simple housewifely tasks, Serina couldn't help the flush of pleasure that spread through her. She, Serina, could make him happy. *She* was what he preferred.

Not only that, but, from the sound of things, Aaron *was* thinking of marrying again some time. Why else would his sister keep trying to find a wife for him? Serina's heart swelled with hope.

'She sounds very sweet. And I don't think I'll come as such a shock at all. I'm much more domesticated than you realise.'

'Domesticated? You?' He laughed. 'I'll bet your idea of domesticated is ringing down and having a Chinese sent up.' Still smiling, he slipped an arm through hers and began leading her down the path towards the car.

'I might surprise you,' she said. 'But truly, Aaron, if your sister's matchmaking irritates you, why put up with it? Why don't you just tell her to butt out, that you will choose your own wife, if and when you decide to remarry?'

Again he laughed, but it had a harsher sound this time. 'My God, the last thing in the world I want to do is get married again. Ever! But try telling that to a woman who's recently found the joys of wedded bliss after fearing she was going to be left on the shelf.'

'Oh?' Serina swallowed, trying to dispel that awful tightness that had claimed her chest at his words. 'Your sister hasn't been married long, then?' she managed to get out.

'A few years now. To one of the doctors who tended my father during his final illness. Gerald had been recently divorced after thirty years of marriage and obviously needed a woman to look after him. Not that he doesn't love Jillian. I'm sure he does. Actually, she's quite a handsome woman for her age.'

They had reached the BMW, where Aaron released Serina's arm to slip the car key into the passenger-door. She just stood there in stunned silence, her mind whirling away. There was no doubting Aaron meant what he'd said about never wanting to marry again. And, for her part, Serina had vowed she would *never* allow herself to be used as a mere means of sexual gratification.

Yet that was all Aaron wanted from her. She'd been fooling herself in hoping differently. She just hadn't wanted to admit he was no different from other men who'd pursued her.

'One more thing,' Aaron was saying smoothly as he retrieved his key and opened the door. 'Just so that you're not caught on the hop, so to speak. This family dinner tonight is to celebrate my birthday. I reached the grand age of thirty-four today.'

'Your *birthday*,' she groaned. 'Oh, Aaron, why didn't you tell me? I would have bought you a present... at least a card...'

She grimaced and shook her head, her eyes dropping to the ground in irritation. Typical man! Didn't he know she would find such a situation embarrassing? Besides, she *liked* giving presents!

His right hand reached out to find her chin, lifting and turning her face so that she was looking up into his eyes. 'I'll settle for a birthday kiss,' he said, his voice dropping to a low, husky timbre.

She stared up at him, eyes wide, her throat swallowing convulsively.

'Don't look so worried,' he murmured, his head bending to taste her lips very briefly. But he didn't stop at one. His mouth bent again and again. Light, fleeting touches of flesh on flesh, full of suppressed passion and an unbelievable eroticism. Serina's heartbeat stopped entirely.

His head lifted and he stared down into her startled eyes. 'Damn, but you're irresistible,' he muttered, and swept her up against him, taking her mouth again, this time with a far greater force.

Her knees started to go from under her and she clutched at his jacket, her bag clattering to the concrete driveway as it slipped from suddenly nerveless fingers. But she didn't notice, her whole awareness now on Aaron's deeper kiss and the devastating effect it was having on her.

As Aaron's mouth moved over hers a definite current shot through her veins, racing up into her head, making it swim madly, rocking her, dazzling her. She couldn't think, the last of her conscious mind swept away by the intoxicating excitement his kiss was evoking in her. Her lips fell open beneath his and his tongue slid into her mouth, hot and moist and wild.

But all too soon his tongue retreated and his mouth was lifting from hers, the feeling of desertion blasting through her soul like a winter wind. She moaned and clung to him, her eyes closed, her face uplifted for more. No man had ever done this to her. All these years...*nothing*! And now this...this ecstasy. She was enthralled, captivated...

He made some sound—a low, animal growl—making her eyes flutter open in a glazed alarm. But then he was giving her what she wanted, his mouth clamping back down over hers with sudden savagery, his arms sliding back around her, pulling her hard against him, squashing her hands between them.

She didn't mind his harshness, rather revelling in the way he was holding her and the way he was ravaging her lips.

But just as she felt that she was no longer a person, merely an empty vessel desperately needing to be filled, a piercing whistle broke the stillness of the air, a knowing, shaming whistle, and Aaron pulled back. Serina gave a whimpering cry, not wanting him to stop, and sagged back into him.

But then the whistle came again and the reality of what she was doing finally sank in. She spun round, her hand coming up to touch her tingling mouth, her eyes pained, her cheeks reddening with embarrassment. A quick sidewards glance showed one of the neighbour's children, a lad of about fifteen, going down the hill on a skateboard, grinning back at them. 'Go for it!' he called out over his shoulder.

'Here,' Aaron said, picking up her bag and pressing it into her limp hand. 'We'd better get moving before we scandalise the whole neighbourhood.'

If there was one thing Serina could count on it was her ability to quickly come to grips with situations. Ten years on her own had produced a certain resilience that a younger girl couldn't have hoped to have. She could appear quite composed while underneath being upset, angry, even as agitated as she was now. Any girl who worked in some of the jobs Serina had worked in —cocktail waitress, entertainment director, motel receptionist— had to be capable of keeping her cool. Sexual harassment, drunken customers, persistent salesmen, jealous wives. All had made life difficult. One learnt to cope. Or starve.

So Serina gathered herself and stepped past Aaron to climb into the car. She slipped on her seatbelt and schooled her face into a calm, composed expression. Any other reaction would be admitting she had been unusually affected by his kisses. To let him know that she was as stunningly vulnerable to him as she obviously was would be to present her body to him on a silver platter.

Serina gave him only a darting glance as he slid behind the wheel of the car. But it was impossible not to notice the pleased, almost smug set to his face. Did he think now that she had changed her mind, that she had just given him the green light for the 'adult' affair he wanted?

A wave of brutal honesty swept through her.

Of course he's going to think that, you little fool.

Serina sagged back into the passenger-seat, closing her eyes in dismay. Her head was whirling, and her body still felt as if she had walked across hot coals. She'd known she was sexually attracted to Aaron— always *had* been—but the intensity of her response had completely thrown her. She'd not only become aroused, but *mindlessly* aroused. If they'd been inside the house, instead of out in the street, they would undoubtedly have ended up in bed.

Serina felt torn by both temptation and her strong sense of personal survival. One told her to forget her pride, to grab for herself the sort of sexual pleasure she had never experienced, nor *dreamt* of experiencing. On the other hand, common sense kept warning not to give in to him, that if she did it would lead to a misery greater than she had ever known.

She'd spent twenty-eight years waiting and hoping for true love. She didn't want an 'adult' affair. She wanted the fulfilment of her dreams, the fairy-tale.

But one look at Aaron's face told her he had long stopped believing in fairy-tales.

She gave a silent groan as Aaron drove off, and hoped that by the time he brought her home later in the evening she would have the courage necessary to do what she had to do.

CHAPTER FOUR

SERINA remained tensely silent while Aaron drove down to the bottom of the hill and smoothly negotiated the busy corner turning on to the Pacific Highway. She might have stayed silent indefinitely, nursing her desolation, but when he didn't continue on the highway which led straight into Gosford, taking instead a back-road that wound a narrow, pot-holed path through an isolated valley, curiosity got the better of her.

'Where on earth does your sister live?' she asked.

'Near Forrester's Beach. This is a short cut. But hell, just look at this road. You could disappear into some of these pot-holes and never be found again!'

'It's all the rain we've been having.'

'As if this area needs more rain,' came his grumbling reply.

And Serina had to agree. The central coast's vegetation growth was normally prolific, the proximity of the surrounding mountains to the semi-tropical coastline creating a type of rain-forest basin. Now, with the above-average rainfall, everything was beginning to look like a jungle, with a jungle's accompanying wildness.

'Hardly the sort of conditions the makers of this car envisaged,' Aaron muttered as they sank axle-deep into another rut.

'Maybe you should go the long way round, back through Gosford.'

'Hmm.' Aaron darted her a wry, sidewards glance. 'Too late now. Once I'm committed to something I refuse to go backwards.'

There was no agreeing or disagreeing, for at that moment an unmistakable thud reverberated through the car and the BMW slewed over to the side of the road, skidding from broken tar into mud before coming to a shuddering halt. Neither of the occupants needed to put their heads out of the window to know what had happened. The back left-hand tyre had succumbed to the hazardous terrain.

Aaron grimaced and thumped the steering-wheel, 'Damn and blast!'

'Never mind,' Serina soothed, her varied travels having engendered an easygoing approach to unavoidable hitches and delays. 'No real damage done. You have a spare, don't you? I'll help.' She was already clambering out.

Aaron did likewise, facing her over the bonnet of the car with a rueful expression. 'Don't be silly, Serina. I can hardly have you slopping around in this mud in your good clothes. Get back in.'

'Certainly not! Your clothes are just as good as mine. Do you have something in the boot we could spread out on the ground beside the wheel? An old blanket or tarpaulin?'

He frowned at her adamant refusal to play helpless lady. 'I think so.'

They both walked around the back of the car and Aaron opened the boot, pulling out a checked travelling rug.

'Better put your hazard lights on,' Serina advised; the evening was getting dark quickly due to some extra cloud-cover.

He gave her a sardonic look. 'You don't like advice but you don't mind giving it, do you?'

'Sorry,' she shrugged. 'Should I just stand around looking anxious?'

'No . . . just beautiful will do.'

She looked down, fiercely troubled by what he could do to her with a few words. It was far too exciting, too seductive, too tempting. Human beings weren't saints and she was definitely only a human being. A type of anger seized her. Why was fate so cruel to her, bringing her back into contact with the man of her dreams, only to find him flawed? She wanted true love, marriage, a family of her own. She didn't want to waste any more of her life on self-destructive relationships. She wanted the real thing this time. Yet all she was being offered was a temporary going-nowhere affair. What angered her most was that she might actually agree to it.

'It's as flat as a tack, isn't it?' she said, kicking the tyre with extra vigour.

'You're not wrong there,' Aaron agreed, bending inside the driver's window to switch on the blinking hazard lights. 'Here . . . I do have a job for you. Hold my jacket.'

He slid out of it, displaying that magnificent physique he'd always had. Serina had to consciously keep her eyes from running over him as he handed her the garment and rolled up his sleeves. But when he'd finished jacking the car up and crouched down to start loosening the nuts—his back to her—her gaze was automatically drawn to him, lingering on the way his trousers stretched tightly across his taut buttocks and hard-muscled thighs. His shirt, too, was straining across his back, and as she stared at him she experienced the most compulsive desire to reach out and put her hands on his shoulders. She did so in her mind, but it didn't stop there. In her fantasy her palms began sliding down across his shoulder-blades, her fingers following his male shape, touching and exploring...

'Want to have a go?' he asked, glancing abruptly up over his shoulder.

She gaped at him, his words bringing a hot flush of guilt till she realised he couldn't possibly have meant what she'd first thought. 'At...at what?' she asked, her voice trembling traitorously.

But he didn't appear to notice, his mind on the wheel and not her fluster. 'At this last rotten, damned nut,' he growled, straightening and stretching, his fingers massaging the small of his back. 'Blasted thing won't budge.' He took his jacket from her and dropped the wrench in her hand. 'You might as well try while I'm having a rest.'

Now, many a jar-lid and bottle-top had given way to Serina's deceptive strength. She took a deep breath, bent and put every ounce of energy she had into her first tug. It gave ground straight away.

'Good lord, you *did* it!' Aaron gasped.

Her face was a perfect picture of *savoir-faire* as she rose to her feet and dropped the wrench back into his stunned hand. 'Naturally. We women are good for more things than making tea, you know.'

'Hmm...I'm sure you are,' he drawled, his eyes going to her mouth.

Serina froze. They were standing very close, their breathing the only sound in the evening stillness of the secluded valley. His eyes grew dark with desire and she suspected that if they weren't where they were, standing on the edge of a road where a car could come along any minute, he would have dragged her to him and kissed her again.

But he turned away, bending over to finish changing the wheel, leaving Serina standing there with her heart in her mouth. How on earth was she going to stop him if he started making love to her at the end of the night? Or, more to the point, how was she going to stop herself?

'All done,' Aaron announced, and stood up to roll the removed flat tyre back round to the boot. Serina gathered up the rug and joined him there.

'I . . . I suppose we're late for dinner now,' she said quietly.

'No doubt about it. Look, don't worry. We'll go to the closest garage and ring Jillian, let her know what's happened while I get this tyre fixed.' He glanced at his watch. 'We should still make it to her place by eight.'

'I hope she doesn't blame me.'

'Why should she?'

Serina shrugged.

'We'd better shake a leg, through.' Aaron added briskly.

It was a hair-raising next few minutes, what with the pot-holes and a sudden summer shower making driving difficult, and Aaron not conceding much speed to either. Serina was quite relieved when the short cut finally emerged on to the main road that led out to the beaches.

'Look, there's a garage,' she pointed out. 'And a phone . . .'

Fifteen minutes later they were on their way again, Jillian having been sufficiently soothed with an explanatory phone call.

'Do men always look at you like that?' Aaron snarled as he drove off from the garage.

'Like what?' she frowned. 'Who?'

'That sleazy little mechanic. He stared at you the whole time you were cleaning your shoes.'

'Oh.' Hardly a new experience for Serina, but perhaps she shouldn't have smiled as she'd asked the mechanic for those paper towels.

But Aaron's annoyance over the mechanic's behaviour was rather the pot calling the kettle black, she thought.

'I can't help it if men look at me,' she said defensively. 'It's irritating sometimes, but what can I do about it? Cover up, like a Muslim woman?'

'Maybe that's not such a bad idea,' he snapped.

'Don't be ridiculous. It's too hot, for one thing. Besides, I shouldn't be punished for men's dirty minds.'

His frown was dark and puzzled, his silence aggravating.

'I thought we were going to Forrester's Beach,' she said as they flew past the turn-off.

Aaron's expletive wasn't exactly obscene, but it wouldn't have passed muster at the dinner table.

'I don't think you're good for my concentration,' he grumbled as he wrenched the car around.

Her glance was dry, a perfect cover for her own inner agitation. 'Perhaps you shouldn't be taking me out, then. Perhaps you should have settled for one of those widows Jillian lines up for you.'

'God, no! They're all mutton dressed up as lamb.'

'But at least you'd be able to concentrate. And the mechanic wouldn't have stared.'

His grin came slowly. 'Much safer all round,' he agreed. 'But awfully boring. Not something that you would ever be, Serina. Exasperating, yes. Frustrating, yes. But boring? Never!'

'I'm so relieved.'

He laughed. 'Are you always so enchantingly sarcastic?'

'Only on Sunday evenings.'

'Now, now, that's a fib. You were in fine fettle last Tuesday on the phone to poor old Rupert.'

'Hmph!'

'No comeback?' he teased.

'Never on a Sunday,' she quipped, aware that their repartee had disintegrated into flirting, but unable to stop. She knew it was madness to encourage him but being with him was like being on a roller-coaster ride over which she had no control.

Aaron reefed the car into a side-street and started heading up a steep incline. 'Give me a quick run-down on your brothers before we hit Jillian's. We're only seconds away from touch-down and I don't want to be caught out in ignorance after saying you were an old, old friend.'

Serina breathed deeply, trying to calm a flutter of nerves at the thought of meeting Aaron's family. 'Rupert's thirty-six now, a high-flying barrister with a practice in Sydney. Married to Vivian, society wife. No children. Philip's into computers. Writes programs, I think. He's thirty-two and married Evonne, a model, last year. No kiddies as yet.'

Aaron released his seatbelt and twisted in his seat to face her. 'Splendidly done. I should hire you to write my reports. Succinct but informative. Now! Much as I would prefer to stay out here with you, I think we'd better go inside. The soup is probably on its third re-heat by now.'

'Was your sister very upset?' Serina asked as they walked together towards the house, which at first glance looked very opulent and large, a multi-level cement and glass structure that followed the sloping land as it dropped back from the road.

'More worried than upset. I think,' Aaron confirmed. 'Christine was the one who was really miffed. I don't see her all that much and she can be very possessive of my time.'

'I can appreciate that,' Serina murmured, thinking about Aaron's daughter in some depth for the first time. Poor kid, losing her mother when she was only a teenager. If Aaron was thirty-four Christine would have to be sixteen. And boarding-school certainly wasn't always what it was cracked up to be.

'Does she like boarding-school, Aaron?'

He shrugged. 'She's never complained, but then she wouldn't. She's a really good kid. You'll like her.'

The front door was suddenly yanked open.

'Thank God you're here at last!'

The man belonging to the booming voice was about fifty-five, with a round pleasant face, thinning grey hair and a shape that bespoke far too many dinner parties.

'Sorry, Gerald,' Aaron apologised.

'Not your fault, old chap. But it's damned hard to keep food both warm and appetising indefinitely. We were supposed to be consuming homemade French onion soup and crispy croutons fifteen minutes ago.' He swung his twinkling eyes in Serina's direction. 'Aah, I do see what you were trying to tell me on the phone the other night, dear boy. A distinct improvement on Jillian's offering the other week, eh, what?'

'Hmm.'

'Serina's the name, isn't it?' Gerald continued with a broad smile.

'Serina Marchmont,' she completed, thinking what a nice jovial person Jillian's husband was but trying to guess what Aaron had said about her on the phone. Something like 'Wait till you see what I'm bringing, old chap. Thirty-six, twenty-four, thirty six, complete with blonde hair and no brains!'

It hardened her resolve to be strong at the end of the evening. 'Should I call you Gerald or Doctor?' she asked.

'Gerald, if you know what's good for you, young woman! None of that stuffy 'Doctor' rubbish around me.'

'Shouldn't we be getting inside?' Aaron suggested somewhat stiffly. He didn't seem to be appreciating the way Gerald was openly admiring her. Too bad, she thought with definite annoyance. You can't have it all, Aaron. Take a *girl like me* out and you have to put up with the drawbacks.

They all bundled into the wide tiled foyer, one swiftly encompassing glance confirming what Serina had first thought of the house. No expense had been spared, from the Persian rug on the floor to the felt-styled wallpaper to the chandelier hanging from the ceiling.

'And about time too,' an impatient female voice said as its owner flung open one of the double doors to the left.

Jillian was indeed a handsome woman, with a strong face, short, sleek ash-brown hair and piercing grey eyes, her imposing figure suited by the wide-shouldered red linen dress she was wearing. Giving Serina a sharp look, she strode forward and kissed her brother on the cheek. 'Happy birthday, darling,' she gushed. 'And this is Serina,' she continued with a tight little smile. 'You're so right, Aaron,' she told her brother, 'she *is* very pretty.'

Serina couldn't bear being talked about as though she were a wax dummy. 'How kind of you to say so,' she returned as though she had been addressed directly. 'But I've never thought of myself as pretty. My mouth is too big, for one thing.'

Gerald cleared his throat rather noisily, and his wife glared at him.

'What's going on out here?'

They all swung around as another man joined them in the foyer. He was nearing forty, Serina guessed, solid, but quite good-looking in a laid-back fashion, with untidy black wavy hair and lazy brown eyes. He was wearing black trousers and a striped shirt rolled up at the cuffs.

'Good grief, Aaron,' he drawled. 'If you're going to be this late for your own birthday dinner the least you can do is get on inside when you finally do arrive.' His eyes found Serina's, dropping briefly to survey her figure before raising a single eyebrow. He wandered over to stand close to Aaron, Serina not missing the surreptitious dig in the ribs. 'Glad to see you finally took my advice, dear chum,' he muttered.

Serina stiffened, wondering exactly what he meant by that remark.

'Do you mind?' Aaron growled back. 'This unfortunate person masquerading as a gentleman, Serina, is my business partner, Craig Everly. Perhaps soon to be my *ex*-business partner,' he ground out, looking daggers at the man. 'But you are right about one thing—we should all be getting in to dinner. Now, where's that daughter of mine?'

'Dad! Where have you *been*?'

A teenage whirl in blue jeans and an enormous white shirt hurtled across the foyer and into her father's arms. 'Happy birthday!' She gave him a big kiss which Serina was glad to see didn't embarrass Aaron.

He hugged the girl back with enthusiasm. 'Thanks, sweetie-pie. Now, how about turning round and meeting our guest? Serina, this is Christine, my energetic daughter. Christine, this is Serina Marchmont, an old friend from my schooldays.'

'Old?' the girl squawked. 'She's not old, Dad, unless she's had a face-lift!'

Serina laughed. The girl was very pretty, with flashing brown eyes and shoulder-length wavy brown hair. 'No face-lift yet,' Serina confessed, thinking Aaron's daughter was delightfully natural. At least the boarding-school environment hadn't made her shy or introverted.

She did, however, have a tendency to chatter away at a speed and effervescence not uncommon in teenage girls. She began telling her father a multitude of things from the cake she had baked that day to the *awesome* present she had bought him. The word 'awesome' figured largely in every sentence.

After a very short time Jillian raised her eyebrows and excused herself, taking Gerald with her to the kitchen to help serve up, but not before leaving strict instructions for Craig to get everyone seated in the dining-room. This he did with great panache, seating Serina next to him on one side of the oval dining-room table, explaining that Christine had wanted to be next to her father. Aaron hadn't seemed too pleased with the arrangement but Serina didn't mind at all. The further she was away from Aaron's disturbing physical presence, the better.

Once settled, she glanced around the large room, admiring Jillian's taste. Predominantly green in décor, the room was very elegant, with exquisite velvet-embossed wallpaper and lovely, gilt-framed pictures on the walls that could only be originals: landscapes of what looked like local scenes.

Jillian bustled in straight away with the croutons and soup while Gerald saw to each person's wine requirements, having a wide selection on offer. Serina finally gave her nod to a claret she knew to be good. Craig and Aaron especially, she noticed, had pricked up their ears like startled hounds when she'd had a knowledgeable exchange with Gerald on the merits of the wine.

She totally ignored their looks of surprise, enjoying a feeling of savage satisfaction, and started up a conversation with Christine, asking her if her father had told her about the house.

'Yes,' the girl enthused. 'On the phone. It sounds terrific, and really I don't care all that much about not having a pool. I much prefer the beach anyway. When can I come over and see it? Tomorrow?'

'Christine,' Aaron rebuked quietly, 'you know I have to go to work tomorrow.'

'Why not come by yourself?' Serina suggested. Infinitely better than with her father, she was thinking. 'I have Mondays off work. I *was* going to spend the day doing some Christmas shopping but...'

'Oh, but I have to do some shopping too, don't I, Aunt Jillian? Serina could help me find something for Dad. You know how hard it is to buy him presents, but I'm sure Serina would know *exactly* what a man would like.'

There was a short, sharp silence, before Aaron cleared his throat and said, 'Well, if she doesn't mind...'

'Not at all,' she agreed quickly. 'Do you know Gosford Library?'

Christine was beaming. 'Yes.'

'I'll meet you on the seat outside at nine o'clock. Catch the shops before they get busy. Then afterwards I'll bring you out and show you the house, then take you home on my bike.'

'A bike!' Jillian looked horrified. 'Surely you don't mean a motorbike?'

'Well, yes, I——'

'I think perhaps,' Aaron inserted smoothly, 'I should get off early and come up and meet you both at the house, then drive Christine home myself.'

Serina sighed inwardly. But she couldn't see any way out of the situation, and she appreciated that some people did worry about motorbikes. Though hers was very small and not at all powerful. Her one comfort was that Aaron could hardly try seducing her in his daughter's presence.

The dinner progressed, the soup being whisked away, replaced by the main course, an excellently prepared carpet-bag steak, the oyster filling particularly mouth-watering. Conversation ceased as everyone attacked the meal with gusto, their appetites having been sharpened by the delay in eating.

When the quiet background music stopped at one point Gerald got up and changed the cassette.

'Aah…Chopin,' Serina murmured, recognising one of the composer's most popular polonaises.

Aaron glanced over at her. 'You recognise *Chopin*?' he asked with an undercurrent of patronising astonishment in his voice.

Actually, Serina was not a genuine classical-music buff, but Paul had been crazy about it, especially Chopin. He had played him incessantly. Nevertheless, she wasn't about to confess this. Let the conde-scending devil think she was an expert!

'Not everything Chopin wrote,' she answered silkily, 'but his *Polonaise in A Major* is one of my favourites. I'm not too keen on his piano sonatas. All three are in minor keys. I much prefer his music when written in a major key. Much more positive and stirring, don't you think?'

'Er—yes,' he agreed. 'I'm sure you're right.'

'Serina's not just a pretty face, is she?' Gerald slipped in pointedly, giving her a conspiratorial smile.

'Certainly not,' Craig drawled, his eyes sliding across to her bust first, then up to her mouth.

Serina was tempted to pour the bowl of soup over his head.

'I don't think she's pretty,' Christine piped up, 'I think she's beautiful.'

This compliment was so sincerely meant that Serina felt herself blushing. For something to say she asked Jillian what was in the carrots and beans to make them so delicious.

'It's just a hint of crushed garlic and cream, mixed in after the vegetables finish cooking,' the older woman explained, though looking pleased, which led to Serina's discussing a similar recipe with her.

'You seem to know something about cooking as well, Serina,' Gerald said. 'What exactly do you do for a living?'

Serina hesitated, glancing across the table to see Aaron watching her with speculative eyes.

'I've done so many things over my working life that I've lost count,' she admitted to the silent, waiting audience. 'You see, I've moved around a bit, trav-elling up the coast of Queensland, taking various positions in the tourist resorts. I did do a course in cocktail-making a few years back and I do prefer to work in that area, where I have some expertise, but over the years I've also been a receptionist, waitress, assistant cook, aerobics instructress, recreational organiser... I even worked as a labourer once,' she laughed in memory, 'carting bricks at a development site.'

'My goodness!' Christine exclaimed. 'How did you manage?'

'She's stronger than she looks,' was Aaron's rueful comment.

Serina met his eyes, hers laughing at the memory of the incident with the tyre. He shook his head at her, and slowly the corner of his mouth lifted into a wry smile. 'A mine of hidden talents, aren't you?' he said.

'Some not so hidden,' came the comment in her left ear, so low that no one else could possibly have heard.

Serina wasn't about to put up with it, though, and leant over to whisper in return, 'Another crack like that, buster, and I'm going to kick you in the shins and pour this claret right down your front. Got it? Now smile, Craig, dear. People are watching.'

Not only did he smile. He laughed.

'Can we join in on the joke?' Aaron said in a voice that could have cut butter.

Serina's eyes jerked up—there was a decidedly jealous light in that hard blue gaze. It astonished her. Could she be wrong about him? Could he be beginning to feel more for her than just lust? Perhaps she had shown him tonight that she had other facets to her person that were worth exploring besides her more obvious ones.

'Serina was merely reminding me to keep my elbows in,' Craig covered expertly. 'No joke.'

'Really,' Aaron said drily.

'Everyone ready for dessert?' Gerald jumped up.

Everyone was, it seemed, though Aaron continued to look at both Craig and Serina with dark suspicion.

The dessert was scrumptious, a passion-fruit sorbet that would have done a chef proud. Serina told Jillian so and the woman warmed to her some more.

When Gerald announced that they would move into the living-room for coffee, Aaron was astoundingly quick to regain Serina's arm and direct her to a two-seater. 'I can see I have to keep a close eye on you,' he muttered darkly, and drew her down next to him. 'You're an incorrigible flirt.'

She turned indignant eyes towards him. 'I am *not*,' she denied, though keeping her voice down.

He put an arm round her shoulders, drawing her breathtakingly close. 'No, I dare say you're not,' he rasped at her ear. 'You don't flirt. You plan every move you make. You're the complete Eve, aren't you? But you're not content with just Adam. You want every man who comes your way to want you.'

Serina's indrawn breath was full of raw pain. In any other circumstances she might have got up and left, but she spied Christine coming into the room with an armful of presents and didn't want to spoil the night for the girl. Still, she aimed on giving Aaron a piece of her mind later.

'Present-time!' Christine announced, and put the gaily wrapped parcels on the coffee-table. Jillian came in at the same time with a tray of coffee and the birthday cake. Serina had no option but to grin and bear the next half-hour of present-opening and cake-eating.

Aaron's gifts were very diverse. An engraved gold pen set from Jillian. A crocodile-skin wallet from Gerald. A hard-cover edition of the new Tom Clancy book from Christine. And a rare bottle of whisky from Craig.

'What did Serina give you?' Craig drawled. 'Or shouldn't I ask?'

Serina wasn't normally thrown by sexual innuendoes. But, after what Aaron had just said, an uncomfortably warm flush started creeping up her neck.

'As we're only just getting reacquainted,' Aaron rejoined smoothly, 'I didn't expect her to buy me anything. The pleasure of her company was a gift in itself.'

'Oh, Dad, how sweet!' Christine exclaimed.

'Almost poetic,' drawled Craig.

'I think you're all embarrassing the girl,' Gerald observed.

'Nonsense!' Jillian laughed. 'Serina's hardly a girl, and not so easily embarrassed, are you, dear?'

'I dare say embarrassment *is* somewhat relative to age,' she stated, 'but I'm not entirely immune yet.' She flicked Craig an icy glare before turning equally chilling eyes towards Aaron. 'I don't like to be a killjoy, but I *am* tired...'

His eyebrows lifted. 'Looks as if I have to take Cinderella home. Well, what time shall I meet you and Christine at the house tomorrow? Will four do?'

Four was agreed upon, and within five minutes Serina was back in the passenger-seat of the BMW and they were on their way.

A further five minutes later, there still hadn't been a word spoken between them. Aaron was the first to crack.

'I take it your silence means I won't be invited in tonight?'

'You take it correctly,' she retorted.

'Why? Because of what I said, or because you've decided you like Craig better? Did he tell you he was divorced while he chatted you up at the table? Planning to have him drop by later, are you? Is that why we left early?'

Serina could hardly believe what she was hearing. 'We left early,' she bit out, 'because you were becoming insufferably offensive. No other reason.'

Aaron glowered. 'Don't go telling me Craig wasn't coming on to you over dinner or that you weren't liking it.'

Serina sighed her complete exasperation. 'Craig wasn't coming on to me and I wasn't liking it,' she informed him crossly. 'If you must know he made some crude reference to my boobs, and I told him if he did it again I'd kick him in the shins and pour my claret down his front.'

Aaron literally gaped across at her.

Finally he threw back his head and roared with laughter. 'Oh, I like that. I really like that!'

'Well, I didn't,' she ground out. 'I found it positively boring. I'm fed up to the eye-teeth with men taking one look at my chest and thinking "sexbomb". You're included in that too, Aaron, though I expected more from you. You used to be a person of some intelligence and integrity. Or so I always thought. I can see I was wrong.'

His face grew serious and he appeared to give her heated remarks considerable thought. 'Look, I'm sorry, Serina. Truly sorry. I dare say I have been guilty of some presumptions about you, not that you haven't taken me to task on a few of them already tonight!

Of course...that doesn't mean your bust isn't very...um...'

She turned on him, eyes flashing. 'One word,' she warned, 'just one word and I'm going to get out of this car!'

CHAPTER FIVE

THEY finished the drive home in silence. Aaron pulled up outside her house, switched off the engine and turned towards Serina. She was astonished to see that he wasn't at all chastened, a faintly amused smile on his face. 'Well, Serina? I take it I'm not to be invited in for coffee tonight.'

She took a deep breath and summoned up all her resources for being both strong and sensible. 'Not tonight or any other night, Aaron. I don't want to keep seeing you on a personal level. We don't want the same things in life.'

He said nothing for the longest few seconds she had ever experienced. 'I don't agree with you,' he said at last in a strained voice. 'But I won't try to dissuade you at this late hour. We'll talk again tomorrow when I pick up Christine. I must insist, however, that you let me see you safely inside.'

Panic set in immediately. 'There's no need. Really . . .'

His mouth thinned into a tight, hard line. 'I beg to differ. The house is in darkness. You live alone in a quiet area. I won't rest properly till I check for myself that there's no one in the house.'

She went to protest again, but he was already getting out of the car. They walked together to the front door, Serina feeling very tense. Once they were inside he checked the whole house, then returned to where she was still standing in the now lit hallway. She was taken aback when he reached out and pushed the front door shut behind her.

'What . . . what do you think you're doing?' she demanded shakily.

He faced her, blue eyes determined. 'I'm going to kiss you goodnight, and I don't want anyone or anything interrupting this time.'

'But . . . but I don't want you to.'

'It's only a kiss, Serina.' Already his arms were sliding around her. 'Don't make a big deal about it.'

Serina stared at his descending mouth, thinking there was no such thing as 'just a kiss' from this man.

She gulped and pressed her lips firmly together a second before his made contact. Immediately his mouth lifted and he lanced her with reproachful eyes. 'Come, now,' he rebuked softly. 'You can do better than that. Don't forget, it *is* my birthday.'

His mouth descended once more.

Oh, God, she thought as his lips moved over hers with tantalising slowness. She squeezed her eyes tightly shut and tried to think of anything but how his flesh felt on hers. Keep your mouth shut, she told herself firmly. A few more seconds and it will all be over.

But it wasn't over in a few more seconds. She sensed the change in him, the sudden flare of desire. His hold tightened, pulling her breathtakingly close. The pressure of his mouth increased, and in the end she couldn't resist, her own lips softening and pouting, then parting. Their tongue-tips met and she trembled.

A groan echoed deep in his throat. His mouth lifted slightly as he sucked in a ragged breath, then swooped again.

This time he was not content with a mere fleeting contact. His questing tongue slid between her lips, deep into the cavern of her mouth, and every nerve-ending in her body leapt. The embers of thwarted passion that had smouldered in her all night from his kisses earlier in the evening were set alight, one by one. It was like being consumed by a small scrub fire, controllable at first. Till his right hand left her back and slid round over her right breast.

Then the flames roared upwards, exploding with a blazing burst of sparks, sending a tortured little cry from her lungs with a wild pounding into her head. Her body shook, her hands fluttering up to push against his hard male chest in panic.

She might as well have been trying to move the Great Wall of China, so ineffectual were her struggles. His only movement, except for the rapid rise and fall of his chest, was to urge her back against the door. Both his hands were under her top now, moving feverishly over her bare skin up to her bust, finding and touching the already hard peaks through the silk of her bra.

He searched for but did not find any front opening clasp and with a groan savagely pushed the garment upwards. Serina flinched with a flash of pain, but then he was touching her and nothing else existed but the feel of her breasts free and naked in his hands. It was so incredibly exciting, her heartbeat so hard and fast, that she thought she must surely have a seizure.

'You have the most beautiful breasts,' he rasped. 'Beautiful . . .' Then kissed her again while he played with them, lightly stroking, then kneading, then rubbing her sensitised nipples till she was making sensuous little sounds deep in her throat.

'I want you, Serina,' he groaned against her lips. 'Let me make love to you…please… Don't say no…'

She moaned in a mixture of indecision and desire, for she had never felt like this before, never been swept away in such a fervour of passion. She wanted to say no, but he kept touching her and soon she was giving a strangled agreement.

Immediately he swept her up into his arms, striding two steps at a time up the stairs. He was halfway along the upstairs hallway when he suddenly stopped. 'You *are* on the Pill, aren't you?' he asked roughly.

She blinked up at him. 'N . . . no.'

His whole body froze. 'Have . . . have you got any contraceptives in the house?'

She shook her head in denial.

Aaron groaned and shut his eyes. Slowly he put her down, then opened his eyes, bitter frustration in their darkened depths.

Serina didn't know what to do, what to say. The passion of a moment ago was already beginning to drain away, replaced by a fierce embarrassment. She turned away from him and began adjusting her clothes with trembling hands.

'I . . . I'm sorry, Serina,' he said with a sigh. 'I'm a bloody fool. Me and my presumptions about you. I stupidly assumed you'd be on the Pill. Thank the lord I asked. My God, if I'd made you pregnant . . .' As she turned back to face him she actually saw him shudder violently.

His reaction startled her till the penny dropped into place and she understood. Of course he'd be upset at the thought of risking an unwanted pregnancy. He'd already made an unmarried woman pregnant once before. Who knew what hell he might have been through when that had happened? Hadn't he made some comment last week about having made dire mistakes while young?

She stared at him and began to wonder what dark secrets lurked behind his unhappy face.

'I'll be better prepared next time,' he muttered.

Aaron's blunt words jolted Serina back to harsh reality and she shook her head. All her fears earlier in the evening had gone within a hair's breadth of being crystallised. *She* hadn't thought about contraception. She hadn't thought about *anything* once he'd started kissing her, touching her.

'There won't be a next time,' she said wretchedly. 'Find someone else, Aaron. Some other woman to satisfy your sexual needs.' She started to tremble with after-shock. 'I ... I'm very attracted to you, but I'm not cut out for this sort of relationship. I tried to tell you. I ... I want more from a man than just sex.'

His sigh was tortured. 'I've really mucked things up tonight, haven't I? First with my accusing you about Craig, then with this fiasco.'

He tried to draw her shivering body back into his arms but Serina staunchly resisted. 'No, Aaron. I won't let you get to me that way. Not twice in one night. I trusted you when I let you come in here and you betrayed that trust. You also tried to trick me the other night when you suggested we get to know each other better first. You're not interested in getting to know me at all, except in the biblical sense.'

His frown was disgruntled. 'You're wrong, Serina.'

'No, I'm not,' she argued shakily. 'People who want to form real relationships ask questions. They also talk about themselves, tell their prospective partner about their past, their troubles, their hopes for the future. But not you. That's because you're not planning any future for us, except in bed.'

His face darkened with her accusation. 'That's not how it is, Serina. The only reason I don't talk about my past is because it's too damned painful to talk about. If it'll make any difference I'll tell you, dammit!'

He spun away, his expression frustrated. He paced to the end of the hall, then whirled and walked back, talking all the way. 'Do you think I had a happy marriage? Do you think I wanted to get married at eighteen? Naomi deliberately got pregnant to trap me. I resisted it, you know, even when she made her pregnancy public knowledge. But then Christine was born, and there she was, a real little human being, and I loved her. So we were married. God, what a disaster! Naomi was...'

He stopped in front of her, lifting both hands to rake through his hair in an agitated gesture. 'Look, I'm sorry, but I really don't want to go into the gory details. Naomi's dead. What point is there in raking over the past? It's the future I want to address and I want *you* in that future, Serina.'

His hands reached out to clasp her shoulders. She flinched, but he made no move to draw her to him.

'I want to make love to you. I want it very badly,' he went on with a directness she had to admire. 'But that's not *all* there is to my feelings for you. I think you're a great girl. I like you enormously. You're charming and intelligent and fun to be with. In fact you're everything I'm looking for in a woman right now. Fair enough that you don't want your life to be a series of one-night stands. Neither do I. But I'm not asking for that. What I am asking is for you to have a relationship with me, a one-to-one long-term relationship. Is that so bad? You want me. You showed me that tonight. I won't hurt you. I'll be good to you.

'Don't turn me down,' he finished softly. 'I *need* you, Serina.'

Her heart went out to him, her soft female giving heart. How could she turn him down? How could she? To be needed was what she wanted almost as much as being loved.

But to agree to an affair—even a long-term one—to put her dream of marriage and a family aside, to settle for second best...

'I...I need more time,' she blurted out. 'I just don't know.'

He gave her a satisfied look that suggested she had already capitulated. Her waffling answer was merely delaying the inevitable.

Serina stared up into his softly smiling face and felt her heart turn over. Emotion swelled in her chest, and suddenly it was all so clear.

He was right, of course. She *was* going to give in. But not for the reason he would probably believe, not simply to satisfy her own sexual needs as well as his. Serina finally realised that she didn't need more time to fall in love with him. What had begun as a schoolgirl crush many, many years ago had already blossomed into a mature adult love, full of all the passion and desire that went with such a love.

Strangely enough, there was no feeling of impending doom with the realisation of her love. It felt good. It felt right. Aaron had always been the man of her dreams, and now that she had this chance with him she wasn't going to let him go. He might only desire her at the moment, but desire could well turn to love in time. She aimed to be around when and if it did.

But, despite having made her decision to become Aaron's lover, Serina reasoned it wouldn't be wise to appear too eager or willing to fall in with his wishes. No one appreciated what they gained easily. She wanted to win his love, not just satisfy his lust.

'Couldn't we just keep on going out together for a little while, without sex?' she asked.

Aaron's expression was drily amused. 'We could try, I suppose. But I can't give any guarantees. Believe it or not, I had no intention of pushing the issue tonight. I was genuinely only going to see you inside safely and kiss you goodnight. And look what happened.'

'No more kisses, then,' she suggested with a softly mischievous smile. 'For a week.'

Aaron groaned. 'All right. A week. But no longer! Good grief, look at the time! It's after one. I'm going to be a wreck by the time I get back to Sydney tonight.'

Serina was startled by the abrupt change of subject, till she accepted that Aaron might want to get out of her company quickly because of his frustration. She felt pleased that he found it a trial being alone with her. How odd, she thought. For the first time in her life she actually *liked* a man lusting after her.

'You're...not staying at Jillian's?' she asked as they both walked back downstairs.

'And face the traffic going back from here on a Monday morning? Heck, no. School's out, remember? This is holiday season. Better I go back tonight. I'll have a clear run and be back at my place in no time.'

'Where is this unit of yours?'

'Double Bay.'

She whistled. 'Very high class.'

'Don't get carried away,' he said, stopping at the front door but making no attempt to touch or kiss her. 'It's company-owned, bought for an investment and to house country clients. I don't mix with the locals.'

'And there I was, thinking I could visit and hob-nob it with Sydney's social set.'

His laugh was dry. 'I think you'd better keep any visits to my unit till after the week is up, don't you?'

She coloured slightly, wondering if he realised she wanted him just as much as he wanted her. 'I'll cook you dinner there one night next week,' she offered.

'And cocktails beforehand? You did say you were an expert at cocktails, didn't you?'

'Definitely. I make a mean Martini.'

'Actually, I've never had a Martini. What are the main ingredients?'

'Gin and vermouth. But you haven't missed much.' She wrinkled her nose. 'They're rather dry.'

He reached out and lightly touched her nose. 'Cute,' he said. His hand drifted down to her mouth before he reefed it away. 'Whoops! Want to smack my hand?'

'Not this time,' she said with a shaky laugh. In truth, when his finger had touched her lips she'd been seized with the temptation to tell him she had changed her mind, that she wanted him to stay, that they would find some way around the contraception business.

Only the promise of a more permanent happiness held her back. That and a strong wish to retain his respect. She felt she had gained that by her stance tonight.

'Four o'clock tomorrow, isn't it?' he checked before he went out the door.

'Yes.'

'Don't forget to lock up,' he threw back over his shoulder.

She waved him off from the doorway, then retreated inside and locked the door.

It was a long, long time before she fell asleep.

CHAPTER SIX

SERINA caught the train into Gosford the following morning, Jillian's reaction to her motorbike making her decide never to risk Christine on the back, even for the short trip from town back to her house. It was only five to nine as she walked towards the seat near the library, but Aaron's daughter was already there, her nose in a book.

'Christine?'

The girl quickly shut what proved to be a colourful best-selling saga and stood up, looking pleased and sheepish at the same time. 'Gosh!' she exclaimed. 'You caught me reading my Christmas present to Uncle Gerald. I bought it a few minutes ago.' She hurriedly stuffed the book back into the plastic shopping-bag.

'Don't worry,' Serina reassured her. 'I do that all the time—buy books for people then read them first. I won't tell if you won't.'

Christine laughed. 'I can see you're not of Aunt Jillian's generation. She'd be horrified. Gee, you look terrific! I love your shirt. And your jeans.'

The shirt was a Ken Done design. Very bright and summery. Her jeans were standard washed-out blue, but modern.

'Thanks. You look pretty sharp yourself.' Which she did, in aboriginal-print board-shorts and matching vest-top. 'Now that we've done our mutual admiration bit,' Serina grinned, 'shall we tackle your dad's present?'

'I'd love to, but I don't even know where to start. I'm totally blank.'

'How much money have you got to spend on him?'

'I could stretch it to fifty dollars.'

'What about a shirt?' Serina suggested. 'You could get a really good one for that price.'

The girl shook her head. 'I'd rather not. I bought him one last year and I don't see him wear it often. My taste and Dad's are not the same.'

'Oh... Then what about a book? No, you gave him one of those for his birthday, didn't you? Which also lets out pens, wallets and whisky.'

'Dad doesn't drink much anyway.'

'He doesn't smoke either, does he?'

'Nope.'

'A regular saint, your dad, isn't he?' Serina quipped with only a smidgen of sarcasm.

Christine only laughed. 'He has his faults, believe me.'

They had begun to walk from the park towards the nearest shops. 'Such as?'

'Well, he's awfully impatient with me when I get poor marks in maths. He can't seem to understand why all people don't have his brilliant brain. He says maths is just logic.'

'Smart people are like that,' Serina remarked, nodding with wise remembrance. Both her brothers had been super at maths.

'Oh, but you shouldn't talk like that!'

'Like what?'

'As if you weren't smart. You are! Look how much you know about music and wine and food and stuff.'

Serina's heart turned over with pleasure. 'I'll get a swelled head if you keep this up, Christine,' she managed to say. 'Not only am I nice, but I dress in terrific clothes and I'm smart. Do you think I should run for prime minister?'

'I'd vote for you if you did. And so would Dad.'

This brought a laugh from Serina.

'Though, come to think of it,' the girl added thoughtfully, 'I think Dad would prefer to be the prime minister. You'll have to settle for first lady. Yes, I like that idea.'

'Really?' Serina chuckled. 'And what would that make you?'

'A sister, I hope.'

'A sis... sister?'

'Well, if you married Dad you'd be sure to have a baby. You're young and healthy and——'

'Christine...'

'Yes?'

They had stopped halfway along the arcade that bisected a long line of small shops. It concerned Serina that Christine might be harbouring false hopes about her father and herself. Much as she desperately wanted to win Aaron's love and perhaps eventually change his mind about remarriage, she was a realist. Things didn't always work out as one wanted. 'I don't think you'd better buy your bridesmaid's dress just yet,' she said quietly.

'Why not? Don't you want to marry Dad? I thought you really liked him.'

'Of course I like him! I... I like him very much, but——'

'And he likes you,' Christine put in eagerly. 'I could tell. He couldn't stop looking at you last night at dinner. Uncle Gerald and Aunt Jillian noticed too.'

Serina sighed her exasperation.

'I suppose you're thinking it's too soon after Mummy's death for Dad to get married again,'

Christine said with a frown, 'but it's been over a year and Dad's still young and good-looking. Besides, I'll be leaving school in two years and I'll probably go to university. Dad will need someone or he'll be terribly lonely. I know he will! But I couldn't stand having one of Aunt Jillian's cronies as my stepmother. The very thought makes me puke. I want someone young and interesting like you. Someone who'd put some fun back into Dad's life. He's been awfully down for such a long time.'

'But, Christine, your father said he has no intention of getting married again. He told me so.'

To Serina's consternation, Christine brushed aside this firm statement of fact.

'You don't want to take any notice of what Dad says about things like that. Aunt Jillian reckons he doesn't know what he wants right now, which is about the only thing I agree with her on. All Dad needs is a push in the right direction, but not into some crafty old widow's arms. Yours would be much better all round.'

Serina rolled her eyes. They certainly didn't know Aaron very well. He was the type of man who, if pushed one way, would go the other out of sheer obstinacy.

'I think we should go buy that Christmas present,' she said hurriedly. 'I've thought of just the thing.'

The big brown eyes lit up again. 'You have? What? What?'

She took the effervescent teenager's arm and steered her forward through the crowd of Christmas shoppers. 'Seeing is worth a thousand words,' she answered brusquely.

'Oh, you're a tease!'

Serina grimaced. This girl had a habit of making *double entendres* without knowing it.

'Did I say something wrong?'

'Not at all. Here we are. The very place.'

They were outside a souvenir shop that sold all sorts of Australian gear and gifts. 'You're not going to buy him a koala bear, are you?' Christine asked, looking doubtful.

'Not this year. Come on. I walked past this shop last week and they had this gorgeous beach towel in it with an Aussie surfing scene on it, sexy girl and all. You said your father likes the beach. He does, doesn't he?'

'Adores it.'

Serina asked the sales assistant about the towel and it was quickly brought. 'Here it is,' the girl said, spreading it out on the counter.

'Oh, it's fantastic!' Christine gasped. 'But...' Her face fell.

'But what?' Serina asked, surprised at anyone frowning over a bikini-clad girl.

'It's seventy dollars...'

'I'll give you the other twenty.' A few days ago Serina might not have been able to make this offer even if she'd wanted to. She'd never been the best of budgeters, and her savings had been decimated by funeral expenses. But probate had been declared last Wednesday, and by Friday her share of her mother's bank savings had been transferred to her account—four and a half thousand dollars.

'But I couldn't let you do that,' Christine protested. 'Dad's very strict when it comes to taking money from people. He would kill me!'

'No, he won't.' Serina reached over and ripped the price tag off the towel. 'He'll never know. Wrap it

up, please. Now, we'll have to choose a card to go
with it . . .'

'It must be great to be confident, like you,' Christine
sighed as they left the shop.

'I wouldn't call you shy, my dear girl.'

Christine's comment set Serina thinking. She was
proud of her confidence, more so because it was not
a natural gift, but an acquired one.

'I know I'm not really shy,' Christine was saying,
'but sometimes I feel so unsure of what to do or how
to act and then I start gabbling away, as I am now.'
She looked crestfallen. 'You never gabble.'

Serina gave her an understanding smile. 'You have
to remember, Christine, that I am twenty-eight. When
I was your age I was far from confident. I was terribly
shy, in fact.'

'Oh, I can't believe that!'

'It's true, I can assure you. People change with
time.' Her mind flew to Aaron for a second and she
hoped that it was true, that he would change, would
come round to wanting what everyone seemed to want
for him. 'Come on, let's go in here and have a cool
drink.'

They walked into a small coffee-lounge, ordered a
couple of chocolate milk shakes and sat down.

'Tell me, Serina,' Christine said after a few sips of
the frothy drink, 'do you think my hair suits me this
way? I'd like to have it cut short and streaked blonde
and permed, but Dad won't let me.'

Serina tried not to look too aghast as she surveyed
the lustrous dark waves that suited the girl to per-
fection. 'Well . . . I've seen lots of girls with hair your
colour try to go blonde and it always turns out a sort
of horrible ginger. So I wouldn't recommend the
blonding part, but of course there's nothing stopping

you having it cut and permed but . . . oh, I honestly wouldn't advise it.'

'Why not?'

'I had my hair cut very short one year when it was the fashion, and a day later I hated it! But I was stuck with it, and it took me three years to grow it again, with bits and pieces sticking out all over the place. I vowed never to have it cut again.'

'Then what about a spiral perm?'

Serina gave the girl's dainty face the once-over, then said, 'You have a small face, Christine, and very thick hair. A perm will almost double the body and totally overwhelm your lovely eyes.'

'Oh . . .' There was disappointment in those lovely eyes.

'I'll bet the girls whose perms you've seen and admired all have fine hair. And probably straight. They need help. You don't. Christine, you have the most beautiful hair I have ever seen and I would hate to see it ruined.'

The eyes perked up, a flush of true pleasure pinking the cheeks. 'You really think my hair's nice?'

'Nice is hardly the word. It's *gorgeous*!'

'My mother had hair like mine.'

'Your mother was a lovely-looking woman,' Serina said softly, afraid that talking about her mother might upset the girl.

'Yes, she was, wasn't she?' A frown settled on her face, which increased Serina's fears. She bitterly wished the subject hadn't come up.

'You know, I've never said this to anyone before,' Christine mused aloud, 'but I don't think Dad was very happy married to Mum. I don't mean he didn't love her. I'm sure he did. He was wonderful to her when she got sick. Very thoughtful and kind and everything. But ... Oh, I don't know ...' Christine expelled a troubled sigh.

Serina felt very sorry for the girl and wanted to help set her worries to rest. 'I don't think you should worry about your parents' relationship, Christine. Nothing's perfect. I know that as a youngster I often wondered why my own mother stayed with my father, whom I thought a pompous, hard man. But now I see that they did love each other, and in their love they accepted each other's faults. Your father would not have stayed with your mother so long if he were terribly unhappy.'

'I suppose you're right.'

'I know I am. Now, what about your other Christmas shopping? Everyone else fixed up?'

'Yes,' she smiled. 'I bought Aunt Jillian a cookbook. Do you think she'll like it?' And she bent down to the shopping-bag propped against the chair and drew out a book especially designed for dinner parties.

'I think she'll be thrilled. OK, you're fixed up, so now you can come and help me buy presents for my two ungrateful brothers and their icky wives.'

'You have brothers? Oh, I'd love a brother.'

'Not mine, you wouldn't.'

They both laughed.

Serina thoroughly enjoyed her morning shopping, with Christine coming with her while she bought both Rupert and Philip the silliest presents. Rupert got an alarm clock shaped like a ball that you threw at the wall to turn the alarm off. She thought it would suit his bad temper. Philip was to receive a practice-putting set for golf, which was diabolically naughty of her, since he was the worst golfer in the world. Both the wives deserved no more thought than perfume, she announced to a greatly amused Christine.

All purchases made, Serina suggested a visit to the post office, where she intended to get rid of her parcels post-haste. Normally Serina might have driven down to Sydney to give them their presents personally, but not after they had dumped her for the holiday season so ungraciously.

But there was nothing post-haste in that post office that day, with a queue out of the door. Everyone and his dog was posting six hundred Christmas cards each! But it reminded her to send one to Paul, so while she waited patiently to be served Serina sent Christine off to buy a card. She was back before Serina had moved ahead three places.

By the time they emerged from the post office they were definitely in need of more sustenance, and Serina treated Christine to a long late lunch. They caught the train back to Serina's station positively bloated with Coke and pizza, and fairly staggered up the hill on the walk home. It had come out hot and humid that afternoon, the morning cloud having passed over, and they were both puffing by the time they turned the corner, only to find Aaron leaning against his BMW, looking cross and heated in a three-piece grey suit.

'It's not four yet!' Christine protested when her father glanced at his watch. 'It's only three fifty-five.'

'What *is* this with your father and time, Christine?' Serina muttered, though the sight of him had set her heart beating. Heavens, but the man looked sexy even when he was cranky!

'Oh, it was a thing Mum had. And I think Dad caught it, like a disease.'

'You two females stop whispering about me,' Aaron grumbled as they grew alongside him. But he surreptitiously winked at Serina.

She pulled a face at him and was just about to make a suitable retort when Christine squealed and started running up the front path and doing her usual running off at the mouth. 'Is this the house? Oh, Dad, it's gorgeous. Oh, I just love the white shutters. It makes it look like a doll's house. And look at the huge front yard! With no trees in it, see? We don't have to worry about putting a pool in the back yard. Look, we could make a courtyard across here and put the pool in the front. Madeline Parson has her pool in the front yard and it's awesome!'

Aaron gave Serina a drily amused look.

'It looks as if you've got a sale.'

'You're prepared to pay what I'm asking?'

His smile was sardonic. 'At this point in time I'd probably pay double if it gets me what I want.'

Her stomach flipped over. Dear God, on the surface he looked so suavely urbane in that business suit with not a hair out of place, but his voice, his eyes . . .

A shiver ran down Serina's spine. She knew that her so-called week's grace was a sham, that the next time she was alone with him there would not only be no stopping, but no holding back of any kind. He wanted it all, and meant to have it.

She was seized by a sudden feeling of nervous inadequacy. Sexually, she wasn't the experienced woman of the world Aaron thought she was. Though Paul had been her lover for over a year, he had been a shy, conservative man. He'd never made love to her either totally naked or with the light on. As for herself, she had merely lain there in his bed, and allowed him to do as he'd willed. She had never been turned on, never wanted any real part of it.

Of course, her feelings where Aaron was concerned were very different. He only had to look at her and she was physically stirred. But as much as she desired him like crazy, would she be able to transform that desire into satisfactory action? She knew the sort of things a woman could do to please a man, but that wasn't the same as having done them. She didn't want to disappoint him...

He must have seen something in her face, for his suddenly tightened. 'Surely you haven't changed your mind, have you?' he said in a strangled voice.

She tried to keep her expression and voice calm. 'No... The fact is...I've decided I don't want to wait a week after all.'

His excitement was tangible and too intense. Far too intense. *Having* her seemed to mean too much to him. It worried her momentarily that it would always override everything else, sweep aside all other aspects of their relationship.

'Come on, Dad...Serina,' Christine called out. 'I want to see my room!'

He took her arm and escorted her towards the house. 'You almost gave me a heart attack then,' he said as they walked. 'You mean I can stay the night tonight?'

Tonight? Her whole being balked at such immediacy. She hadn't realised till that moment that she *did* need more time. A day or so at least. 'Not tonight, Aaron,' she said with a firmness she wasn't feeling. 'I'm busy. Ring me late tomorrow during the day and we'll make plans.'

He sighed, then darted her an admiring glance. 'You're a very together lady, aren't you? And very independent.'

'I suppose so,' she admitted. 'I've lived by myself for a long time.'

'Where are you going to live if I buy this house?'

Serina's heart gave a lurch. 'I . . . I'm not sure.' She hated the thought of moving out of the house. Damn those selfish brothers of hers! she thought with a burst of bitter anger. They didn't really need the money, and it meant so much to her to be here at home after years of wandering from place to place with no real roots.

'Don't worry,' Aaron whispered in a voice vibrating with suppressed desire. 'I'll help you find a nice little place somewhere close, where we can be alone together as much as possible.'

Serina tried not to let his words eat into her. But why didn't he want her to live with him, she agonised, to share his life and his daughter with her? Why did he want her separated off, like a secret mistress? It wasn't as though he were married.

Married . . .

Not for the first time Serina wondered what his marriage had really been like, whether his love for Naomi had survived her trapping him as she had. It didn't seem so. Why else would he be so vehemently opposed to remarrying? Christine had revealed doubts over her parents' happiness that very day. Aaron himself had been very distressed last night when he'd briefly touched on the subject. His reactions, however, definitely put Serina off asking him any more direct questions.

Yet the answers to his present attitude towards relationships had to lie with his marriage. Maybe in time she would be able to put the pieces of the puzzle together. Till then she just had to trust her instincts about Aaron; that underneath he was a good man, a caring man. She also had to believe his claim that he would never hurt her.

'I'd like that,' she said in acceptance of his offer, and deliberately ignored the doubts still lingering inside.

CHAPTER SEVEN

CHRISTINE loved the pink bedroom, loved the house, loved everything, and insisted her father buy it then and there! Aaron laughed and told her that he would inform his solicitor in the morning and have the contracts exchanged as soon as possible. But that didn't satisfy Christine. In the end Aaron rang his solicitor from the house and got things moving straight away, then Serina rang her brothers and informed them of the sale.

Aaron had made one condition, however. He would pay the price they asked provided the furniture came with the house. Serina found it surprising that he had disposed of all the furniture acquired over years of marriage when he'd sold *his* home, but she said nothing. After what he'd told her the night before and what Christine had said today she'd begun to believe that his marriage to Naomi had not been the dream marriage of star-struck teenage lovers she'd always believed. More a nightmare, perhaps.

Rupert and Philip were delighted with the sale, and even remembered to wish Serina an early happy Christmas. They condescended to offer to have her to visit one day after they'd returned from their cruise, which didn't mollify her hurt feelings at all, but did make her glad she hadn't been too mean to send them any gifts.

When everything was settled Aaron suggested, since it had turned swelteringly hot in the last hour, that he take them all to the beach for a swim. He had, he said, brought his board-shorts with him and it was easy enough to drop into Jillian's on the way and get Christine's cossie.

An hour later saw Serina and Aaron stretched out on towels on Forrester's Beach after a cooling dip. Christine was still in the water, having run into a girlfriend of hers. The oldies—as she laughingly called them—were both lying on their backs, enjoying the sun. Thanks to daylight-saving, it would remain shining till well after seven.

'Mmm,' Aaron murmured, turning over on his stomach and propping himself up on his elbows to stare down at her. 'I like the view. Twin mountain peaks.'

Serina's insides tightened. She knew what he was referring to, how the cold sea-water had turned her nipples into hard little pebbles. She also knew what he was trying to do: use words to arouse her. Perhaps he had not given up hope yet of spending tonight with her.

But Serina was still determined to keep some control over the situation. She didn't want Aaron to ever know the power he had over her. Such power, she worried, was bad for a relationship. Her father had had too much power over her mother. Much as Serina loved and wanted Aaron, she refused to become a too willing slave to his wishes.

She flicked a reproving eye up at him. 'You're not staying the night tonight and that's that!'

He sighed dramatically and rolled back over on to his back, giving Serina a full frontal view of his body as he did so. She gulped. Truly, the man had no right to be so formidably armed, no right to have such a great body all round. His broad-shouldered bronzed male torso and long muscular legs looked as though they should have belonged to a twenty-year-old life-saver, not a thirty-four-year-old accountant.

'Then when *can* you get a night off work so that we can be together?' he demanded testily. 'Alone!'

The time for procrastinating was over. There was no real problem getting time off work. She was employed on a casual basis, and could have all the time off she wanted, provided she found someone else to take her place. And she knew of a university student who worked with her occasionally and would appreciate the extra money over the holiday break.

'How about Wednesday,' she suggested, then added smilingly, 'or Thursday, or Friday? Or all three of them? I could get a week off if you like, but I'll have to show up tomorrow to make the arrangements.'

'Fantastic! I'll take you out to dinner and dancing on the Wednesday night, then install you in my unit as my private house-guest for the rest of the week.'

He rolled towards her again and was about to kiss her when Christine came racing up the sand, shouting, 'Dad! Dad!'

They both sat up abruptly and stared at where Christine was pointing out to sea. 'Dad, I think that man out there's in trouble.'

Both Serina and Aaron jumped to their feet, peering out into the choppy surf. Every now and then they could just make out a single surfer, floundering way beyond the breaker-line, a tired arm waving his distress.

'I think he's caught in a rip. You'll have to do something, Dad. There aren't any life-savers around. There isn't even anyone here with a proper surfboard.'

'Oh, God,' Aaron groaned, but immediately began sprinting towards the surf, dashing in and diving under the first wave with an amazing turn of speed.

Serina ran after him to stand anxiously waiting at the water's edge, her heart pounding as she watched Aaron, though this time with fear. The swell had grown even further in the last hour, a stiff northerly breeze whipping up the waves, and the man he was trying to rescue was easily a hundred and fifty yards out.

'What's wrong?' an old lady asked, one of a small crowd that was already gathering.

'Some bloke's in trouble,' a teenage boy answered. 'This lady's husband's gone out to rescue him.'

Serina didn't bother contradicting his assumption, all her attention on Aaron as he disappeared again under a huge wave. Not only would he probably never be her husband, but maybe, within the next few minutes, she might lose the chance for him to be anything to her at all. The sea was a treacherous place. Many people drowned in it every year.

'Please, God, keep him safe,' she prayed aloud.

'You don't have to worry about Dad,' Christine put in proudly. 'He was a champion life-saver in his younger days. Won a lot of competitions.'

'Really?' someone said. 'What's his name?'

'Aaron Kingsley.'

'Hey, I remember him!'

'He won the Australian Iron Man title when he was seventeen,' Christine informed everyone, 'and every year for the next seven years.'

'But that was ten years ago,' Serina reminded Christine in an anxious voice.

All the colour drained from Christine's face. 'You...you don't think anything could happen to Dad, do you?'

Serina saw the girl's instant panic and quickly wiped the worry from her own face. 'Of course not. As you said, love, once an Iron Man, always an Iron Man.' And she put a reassuring arm around the girl's shoulders.

'Yes . . . yes, of course.'

Both of them remained nervously silent as they watched Aaron take ages to get to the man. The rip must have been vicious, for it took him even longer to get back and he was obviously exhausted by the time he staggered into the shallows and handed the victim over to some eager helping hands.

'Oh, Aaron,' Serina cried, racing over to scoop a supporting arm around him as he staggered from the water, her free hand pushing the hair back from his eyes.

He leant against her for a second, their eyes locking. Serina's defences were totally down now, and as she gazed at him with a wealth of relief and affection she realised that she loved this man so deeply, so irrevocably that she would be his, in whatever capacity he wanted, for as long as he wanted. It was as simple as that.

'I'll rescue a stupid damned fool every day,' he gasped, chest heaving. 'If it makes you look at me like that.'

'Gosh, Dad, you were wonderful!' Christine gushed, giving him a hug and a kiss. 'I told Serina you'd be all right. She was worried, but I wasn't.' She gave Serina a sheepish look. 'At least not very much . . .'

Aaron tried to laugh but immediately choked, his breathing still very laboured. 'Hell, I'll have to work out some more after this. I'm well and truly——'

'Exhausted,' Serina finished for him, suspecting that he was about to come out with a much more colourful expression.

He looked at her and grinned. 'Bushed, I was going to say.'

'Sure,' she grinned back.

'I'll go get you a towel, Dad,' Christine offered, and took off up the sand just as two little boys ran up to them. 'Gee, mister, you were terrific!' one of them exclaimed.

'A hero! Just like in the movies!' the other one added.

'Arnold Schwarzenegger, watch out,' Aaron muttered under his breath.

'More Mel Gibson, I think,' Serina returned warmly. 'Or Harrison Ford.'

'Hmm. That's pretty handsome company you're putting me in, sweetheart. Next thing you know you'll start wanting me to make love to you.'

Serina gave him a sardonic glance. 'What do you mean...*start*?'

He grimaced. 'You do pick your times. I couldn't do it now if you paid me.'

'Good,' she pronounced.

'Why good?'

'Because we're going to wait till Wednesday.'

He groaned. 'I could have a little rest, you know, get my strength back.'

'No.' She was firm. 'I want it to be as perfect as it can be. First of all I'm going to the doctor tomorrow and see to certain matters. I'd like to take care of the contraception myself, if you don't mind.'

'You won't get any arguments out of me on that score,' he said with a flash of appreciation.

'Here's your towel, Dad!'

Aaron took the towel from his daughter, wiped his face, then wrapped it around his shoulders. 'The man's OK, isn't he?'

'Right as rain,' Christine said. 'He's already sitting up and asking everyone where the bloke who rescued him is.'

'Let's get out of here, then,' Aaron suggested, 'before I have to go through all that gratitude routine.'

'You should let him thank you,' Serina frowned. 'He'll feel rotten if he doesn't get the chance. Look, he's coming over now.'

'Oh, God . . .'

'He did *what*?' Jillian exploded. Shocked eyes moved from Christine to Aaron to Serina and back to Aaron. 'You silly man! You're not as young as you used to be, you know. You might have drowned!'

'But I *didn't*. Look, I'd like to go take a shower and put some dry clothes on. I'm feeling a trifle waterlogged.'

'Me too,' Christine said. 'What about you, Serina?'

'I'll be OK till I get home.' She was quite dry and had pulled on a knee-length black and white print beach shirt over her costume, her feet covered in her black sandals.

Alone with Jillian in her spacious kitchen, Serina was treated to an amused glance. 'The things some men will do to impress a female.'

'Aaron doesn't need to do anything to impress me,' Serina replied truthfully. 'I was already impressed.'

Jillian was startled for a moment, then she smiled. 'You really care about him, don't you?'

She nodded. 'But don't tell Aaron. He'd feel smothered.'

Jillian gave her a sharp look. 'How clever of you to sense that. You know what? I think you're just the girl for Aaron. Just the girl. I didn't think so when I first met you. I thought you might be . . . well . . . the clinging-vine type. But you're not. You're just what Aaron needs,' the other woman concluded.

'Which is?' Serina asked carefully.

'An independent woman. He must find you a breath of fresh air after Naomi.'

Serina couldn't let this opportunity go by without trying to find out a few more answers to the puzzle of Aaron's marriage. 'Tell me about Naomi, Jillian. I did ask Aaron, but he doesn't want to talk about her, or their marriage.'

Jillian turned up her nose. 'I daren't wonder. The girl was far too intense, too obsessive in her love for him. Quite neurotic really. Madly jealous too, of course. Not just of other women but everything and anything that held his interest, or his affection. I even think she sent Christine away to boarding-school to get the girl out of the house so that she could have Aaron all to herself.'

'But . . . that's *awful*!' she exclaimed, though parts of the puzzle were slotting into place.

'What's awful?' Aaron said as he strode into the room, looking refreshed and marvellous in crisp white shorts and a navy short-sleeved shirt.

'The price of gin, darling,' Jillian improvised, giving Serina a conspiratorial look.

'Yes,' Serina joined in, admiring Jillian's quick thinking. 'I was just saying I could whip you all up a few cocktails, which led us on to the rising price of alcohol in general.'

'Don't make any drinks for me,' he returned. 'I have to drive you home later, remember? I never drink and drive. Where's Gerald, by the way?'

'Still at the hospital,' his sister answered. 'You lot staying for tea?'

'I really should be getting back to Sydney,' Aaron said, 'but I suppose I could stay for a quick snack.'

'A quick snack it is!'

The quick snack lasted over two hours, but finally Aaron drove Serina home.

'I like your sister,' she said as she stood at the front door, determined not to let Aaron in. 'And Christine, of course.'

'They like you too, which doesn't surprise me. You're very likeable.' He grinned at her, then added, 'Are you sure you don't mind catching the train down on Wednesday?'

Serina smiled. She had thought she had already convinced him that to drive up to Gosford to collect her after he finished a long day at the office was crazy.

'Now, Aaron, don't be silly. I've been catching trains and looking after myself for years, and I'm not hung up on convention. I won't get lost and I won't be late,' she reassured him. 'I'll be there at six. On the dot. On the seat closest to the ladies' rest-room.'

'Six,' he repeated. 'I'll be there.'

Oh, Aaron, she thought as she saw the excited anticipation in his eyes. I hope everything does turn out perfect. I hope . . .

No! I won't start hoping for too much just yet.

He went to kiss her but she put a gentle hand over his mouth. 'Wednesday,' she whispered.

He groaned. 'The next two days are going to be hell. Go inside and lock the door, for God's sake.'

Within seconds of her doing so she heard the car start up and he was accelerating away. She leant her back against the door, a study in deep thought as the picture of the man who was Aaron Kingsley gradually came into focus.

He was still a bit blurred around the edges, but by and large Serina could see why he was acting as he was. She could also see that if she wanted to win his love she would have to be the complete opposite of his wife: a giver, not a taker; a sharer, not a selfishly greedy possessor.

Fortunately, her life so far had formed her into an independent, easygoing person, which both Aaron and his family had already commented upon. All she had to do was keep on being her natural self.

Serina went up to bed that night, full of romantic optimism. It was a false optimism, however. She would have done better to dwell on those blurred edges, to remember that there were still many things she did not know about the man she had just agreed to go to bed with in two days' time.

CHAPTER EIGHT

SERINA checked the station clock again. It was two minutes later than it had been the last time she'd looked. Six twenty-six.

Where *was* Aaron?

The thought that he might stand her up had never entered her mind. So where *was* he? She hoped he hadn't had an accident.

She searched the sea of faces around her, but it was peak hour at the station, with people milling everywhere, rushing to and fro to the many platforms and their waiting trains.

Many a time she found herself catching a man's eye with his giving her a speculative stare back, whereupon she would have to deliver a cool look and glance quickly away. That was the nuisance of getting herself all dolled up.

And she *was* all dolled up, both inside and out. No way was Aaron going to be disappointed with her appearance, that was for sure. She had spent most of Tuesday shopping and most of today turning herself out as perfectly as possible.

The black linen suit she had on had set her back a pretty penny but she didn't care. She felt good in it. It looked extra smart, the straight skirt and button-through no-sleeve, no-collar lined jacket showing her shapely figure to advantage without emphasising her bust. Which was just as well, since she wasn't wearing a bra, her undies consisting of nothing but a scandalously erotic black lace teddy. This time, too, she wore no stockings, partly because it was hot, but mostly because she thought her long tanned legs looked just as good naked, especially after she had had them waxed then rubbed oil into them till the golden skin was glowing and soft.

She had dithered for a while over her hair and make-up but had decided in the end to go for broke. So she had left her hair down, only the sides caught up with black combs to show sexy gold hoops in her ears, the rest trailing down her back in a mass of unfettered waves. A bronze gloss shimmered on her full mouth, her eye make-up equally dramatic with a smoky-blue eyeshadow and lashings of black mascara to give her big blue eyes a more exotic and mysterious look.

Bu all these preparations and pamperings would be wasted if Aaron didn't show up!

Serina was still frowning away when she spotted him in the distance, waving madly as he hurried towards her through the crowd. She was on her feet and practically running before she realised how revealing her actions were. Hardly the sophisticate. So she slowed down and greeted him with a cool smile. 'Your watch stop, handsome?'

He stared down at her for a second then swept her up into his arms, kissing her soundly.

'Aaron!' she protested, pulling away from his crushing embrace to look agitatedly around.

'I was afraid you wouldn't wait,' he growled under his breath, and drew her back against him.

'Well I was getting a teensy bit worried, knowing your penchant for punctuality,' she said, trying to control her body's ·response to his nearness and ardour. A silly and futile waste of time. At first sight of him the world had become a dizzyingly marvellous place.

'You wouldn't believe it!' he pronounced irritably.
'I came out of the office in plenty of time. I was even
going to dash home and freshen up before coming
here. I thought the traffic on the bridge seemed unduly
heavy, but to my utter disgust it ground to a complete
halt.'

'An accident?'

'Not quite. Two lanes had been closed temporarily
due to work on the under-harbour tunnel, but on top
of that there was an environmentalist demonstration
to do with harbour pollution right in the middle of
the Harbour Bridge, at peak hour! My God, the
bedlam. I've been stuck in the traffic since before
five!'

'Poor Aaron,' she soothed.

His lips curved back into a relieved smile. 'All's
well that ends well. You waited. You're not even
angry.'

'Aaron, you're only half an hour late. That's
nothing.' But then she remembered his neurotically
jealous wife and wondered if Naomi had given him
hell a few times about being late. 'You know, you
really should learn to loosen up a bit,' she tossed off
nonchalantly. 'Type "A" people are good candidates
for heart attacks, and you're definitely Type "A".'

'And what are you? Type "C" for casual and
carefree?' he teased, taking her carry-all and edging
her through the crowd towards the main exit.

'No,' she returned with a wry laugh. ' "T" for
thirsty. It's darned hot in here.'

'Come on, then. My car's parked down the street,
and my place is only ten minutes away. We'll go there
and you can have a drink while I change, then we'll
saunter down to the Italian restaurant I've booked us
into. It has this intimate little dance-floor and some

sexy violin players so that I can get you in the mood before bringing you home for some serious love-making.' His eyes swept over her as they walked underneath the wide archway that led outside. 'Not that I need any of that to get *me* in the mood,' he added hungrily. 'You look good enough to eat.'

She thought she did well not colouring, and he couldn't, after all, know what his words had done to her pulse-rate. 'You're such a flatterer, Aaron,' she drawled. 'Just like your daughter.'

He chuckled. 'And you're so charmingly droll sometimes. Jane Austen would have loved you.'

'Oh? Are you planning to play Darcy to my Elizabeth?'

He blinked at her.

Serina gave him a 'not again' look. 'Aren't poor little cocktail waitresses supposed to have read *Pride and Prejudice*?' she couldn't help mocking. 'If you like we can pretend I saw the movie. Which I have, several times.'

To give him credit, he recognised his own conde-scension and looked annoyed with himself. 'I'm sorry, Serina, that was awfully patronising of me. Again.' He stopped and drew her free hand up to his mouth, kissing her fingers. 'Forgive me?' He turned her hand over and stretched out her fingers, then put the out-stretched palm to parted lips, the tip of his tongue stroking the warm centre in a wet, sensuous circle.

'Of course,' Her voice was immediately strangled. She'd had no idea that the kissing of a palm could be so arousing.

'You know, you really are a remarkable woman,' he murmured. 'You're continually surprising me, in every way...'

He was far too close in a place that was far too public. 'If you don't get me back to that place of yours pretty soon you'll be even more surprised,' she said, her heart racing as much as her words. 'I will faint dead away at your feet from dehydration.'

He grinned. 'Not something else?'

'Definitely not.'

'If you say so. Not far to go to the car now.' He kept holding her hand as they walked on, his eyes continuously flicking her way. 'Great suit,' he finally said.

'It's new.'

'Mmm. I especially like the buttons down the front. They look wonderfully large and easy to undo.'

Despite all her resolves to act cool, her face flamed.

'I've embarrassed you,' he said, surprised.

'Perhaps.'

'You astound me.'

'I astound myself sometimes,' she said with a dry self-reproach.

'Ah, now, that's more like my Serina. I'll bet you could cut a guy to ribbons if he got out of line with you.'

'Do you think so?' Serina countered archly. She wasn't liking the flavour that had come into the conversation. Aaron was making her sound unshockable and hard. Was that how he saw her?

They drew alongside his BMW and he unlocked the passenger-door, throwing her a frowning glance. When he straightened he took her by the shoulders and looked down at her with worried eyes. 'Don't go cold on me, Serina.'

Impossible, she thought bitterly. It had gone too far for that. 'I'm just nervous. And if you say that surprises you, Aaron, I'll hit you.'

His laugh was soft and gentle. 'You know what? So am I . . . a little.'

She blinked her surprise. 'Are you?'

'I wouldn't be at all . . . if I didn't care about you, Serina.'

It was what she needed to hear, the tender words evoking a rush of love throughout her. Suddenly her whole being was focused on his closeness, his hands on her shoulders, his heart a hair's breadth from hers, and she wanted him to make love to her very, very much.

'Let's not wait till after dinner, Aaron,' she rasped. 'Take me home to bed now.'

His hands closed tightly over her shoulders for a second, his eyes flashing. 'Right,' he muttered, settling her into the car and striding round to climb in behind the wheel with flattering speed.

He darted her a burning glance as he fired the engine. 'Not a word,' he said. 'Not if you want me to get us to my place in one piece. The traffic is rotten and you've just shot my concentration to pieces.'

His concentration was shot to pieces!

Serina leant back in the passenger-seat and closed her eyes. All she could think about was how quickly he had rendered her in a state of mindless excitement and submission the other night with a couple of kisses and caresses. She tried to remember how it had felt with his hands on her naked breasts, tried to imagine what it would be like to have his mouth there, suckling at her flesh like a greedy infant.

Her whole insides contracted with the thought, her nipples hardening against the silk of her underwear. They were still that way when Aaron eventually spoke again.

'Here we are.'

She opened her eyes. And opened. And opened them.

Aaron's apartment block was definitely a shock. Serina had only been joking when she'd made a comment about Double Bay's being so high class. Yes, there were hundreds of expensive units there, and many harbourside mansions. But there were also a lot of older streets and buildings which housed pensioners and workers alike.

Serina had imagined a modest brick building housing units suitable as a stop-over for business clients and such, since it was company-owned.

But the block of units into whose underground car-ports Aaron was swinging his BMW was not only ultra-modern but ultra-ultra-classy. It sank in immediately that Aaron was far richer than she had realised, a conclusion that grew when he took her past the computerised security system in the foyer and up the elegant lift to the tenth floor, where the doors whooshed open on to a red-carpeted corridor.

The silence was especially telling. Not a whisper of traffic sounds filtered through the walls. Very, very few buildings were sound-proof like that. And only very wealthy, successful people owned them.

Serina had met many wealthy, successful men at the various tourist resorts she had worked in. In the main she hadn't liked them. They'd been ruthless and tough and incredibly self-centred.

As she stood there, watching Aaron unlock the door to his unit, her mind flew back to her impressions of him when she'd first seen him in the restaurant just over a week ago, and an uneasy shiver ran up and down her spine.

Had he lulled her into a false sense of security by having her meet his family, then soothing her just now with sweet words of caring? Was she being foolish and naïve, giving sex in the hope of winning love when love wasn't there to be won? Hadn't she realised the very first day she'd seen Aaron that he was no longer capable of loving a woman? What had changed? Nothing...

Except herself.

She had changed. She had fallen in love with him, which was why she was at this moment walking into his apartment, why she was shortly going to allow him to undress her and use her body, and why, God help her, she was probably going to enjoy it more than anything she had ever done.

The door shut quietly behind her and before she could say a word or do anything he was drawing her into his arms and kissing her. But perhaps because of her recent train of thought she could not bring herself to relax, her lips remaining tense and closed as his mouth moved almost questioningly over hers.

He pulled back, frowning.

Instantly she felt guilty and touched his lips, smiling. 'I guess I'm still nervous,' she excused. 'Give me a minute or two.'

She spun away then and pretended to look around, starting with the spacious marble foyer they were standing in. She walked over to the antique gilt hall stand, tidied her hair in the matching mirror, then went over and looked at the enormous, extraordinarily healthy-looking palm nestled in one of the corners, so lush and green that Serina decided it had to be artificial. Till she touched the leaves. 'It's real!' she exclaimed.

Aaron smiled at her surprise. 'I'd take credit but I can't. This is a serviced apartment which includes the rental and care of the plants.'

Serina wandered from the foyer into the combined L-shaped lounge-dining area which was the epitome of understated elegance. White walls, beige curtains, fawn carpet, two ivory leather sofas, the same ivory leather on the dining chairs. 'Very swish, Aaron,' she complimented. 'Being a tax accountant must pay well.'

'That depends,' he said. 'Craig and I have worked hard for what we've got, and I've had some luck with my private investments.'

'Maybe I should get you to advise me on what to do with my share of the house money. I was going to buy myself a small unit somewhere.'

'Real estate is always a good investment,' he agreed, walking with her as she made her way out on to the balcony that lay beyond the glass dining table. 'In another few months you should be able to pick up a bargain. The market's on the way down, though the Gosford area will always be in pretty high demand. You know, Serina, I'd like to buy a unit for you. Or, if you prefer, pay the rent.'

They were standing together at the railing, looking over at the small park that was across the road. A few children were playing on the swings. In the distance the city lights were beginning to blink on with the coming dusk. 'I like paying my own way,' she said without visible rancour, though inside dismayed and annoyed.

But it was *herself* she was annoyed at, not him, for ever pretending this wasn't what it was always going to be. A man—a rich man as it turned out—setting up a mistress somewhere to be at his sexual beck and call.

'I'm going to have a shower,' he said. 'I won't be long. Perhaps you'd like to make yourself a drink while I'm gone to help relax you. You look very tense.

Come on, I'll show you where I keep the alcohol.' He took her hand and drew her back inside, pointing to an antique cocktail cabinet. 'There are glasses and all sorts of spirits in here. Mixer drinks and ice in the fridge. The kitchen's beyond that sliding door. The guest bathroom, the door nearest the foyer. I take it you went to the doctor and fixed that other matter up?'

'Yes.' She didn't look at him. She couldn't.

She heard his slightly frustrated sigh. 'Make yourself at home. I won't be long.'

She herself sighed in relief once he'd actually disappeared into the bedroom.

But Serina didn't make herself a drink. Instead she wandered back out to the balcony and the cooling breeze that was coming from the nearby water. She felt close to despair. To have waited so long to fall in love, only to find her love was going to be wasted . . .

She leant against the railing, and her attention was gradually drawn by one of the little girls playing in the park opposite. The little minx had just gone down the slippery dip, shooting off the end and landing in a puddle, soiling her dress. Her mother raced over, picked her up and scolded her, but no sooner had the woman turned away to speak to one of the other mothers than the child immediately went back and did the same thing again.

It struck Serina that her own behaviour wasn't much different. Getting sexually involved with Aaron was a bit like that child's climbing back up again on to the slippery dip. The little girl did so because it was exciting, because the thrill far outweighed the trouble that came at the end. She didn't really think about the puddle, or the scolding, till afterwards. No doubt she was regretting her actions now that her mother was giving her a good hard whack on the bottom. There was nothing but tears now, any pleasure forgotten...

'You didn't make yourself a drink,' came the reproving comment behind her.

She spun round to find Aaron standing in the doorway to the balcony, a navy blue towelling robe covering what she supposed was a disturbingly naked body. He was rubbing his hair dry with a fluffy cream towel. 'I'll do it for you.' He tossed the towel over his shoulder, then strode back across the dining area and flung open the doors of the cabinet. 'What would you like?' he called out. 'Gin and tonic? Vodka and orange? Whisky and dry?'

'Would you have some cherry brandy?' she asked, and stepped back inside from the balcony.

He bent down and peered into the rows of bottles, the action parting the garment across his bare thighs. Serina swallowed.

'Yes...here's a small bottle.' He stood up, the red liqueur in his hand, the robe falling back modestly into place. 'Going to make up a concoction, are you? Do you think I'd like it?'

'It's very sweet,' she warned.

'Not for me, then. I think I'll have a bourbon.' He pulled out a bottle of Jim Beam.

'Christine tells me you don't drink much.'

His eyebrows lifted as he poured himself a healthy swig. 'She's a talkative little miss, isn't she? I wonder what else you know about me?'

'You're terrific at maths.'

'True...but she's not completely right about the drink. I've been known to have a few, just not in front of my daughter. I'll get some ice. And what else do you need for the cherry brandy?'

'I'll come with you and see what you've got.'

The kitchen was located to the right of the dining-room with a fold-back partition above the servery counter that changed one wall into an open breakfast-bar. Again the colours ran to neutrals, cream cupboards, brown cork tiles on the floor, white appliances and cream marble surfaces.

Aaron topped his drink up with water and ice. Serina selected some tonic water but made her drink very strong. She decided she did need relaxing, for Aaron's state of undress had quickly focused her mind back on why she was here.

She shivered with nerves and excitement, then gulped down her drink, searching perhaps for Dutch courage to actually do what she was suddenly wanting to do. It felt so shocking, so alien to the Serina of old.

But then she remembered that she loved Aaron. It wasn't just sex that was sending these bold desires into her mind. It was the wish to please him, to show him with actions, not words, how much she loved him, futile as that might be. Slowly she lowered her empty glass to the sink, aware that her heart was thudding in her chest like a jack-hammer.

'You drank that rather quickly, didn't you?' Aaron remarked in a low voice.

She turned her head and looked at him, so handsome, so strong, so...male. He returned her gaze, his eyes watchful and narrow.

This is it, Serina. You've climbed up on to that slippery dip and you're looking down the slide, still holding on tightly, knowing there's that puddle at the end, weighing up if it's all worth the inevitable outcome.

A wry little smile came to her lips. Silly Serina. As if it were ever in doubt. It was just a matter of your mind coming to terms with the decision your body made the moment he walked back into your life.

Now don't be a coward, darling. Do what you have to do and to hell with it all!

Slowly but determinedly, she began walking towards him on her black high heels, head proud, shoulders squared. He was looking at her with an almost wary, questioning look in his eyes, his drink hovering at his mouth.

'Can I help you?' he smiled.

'No,' she murmured. 'Just keep drinking.'

But when she untied the sash of his robe and slowly eased the sides apart he definitely stopped drinking. He literally froze when her hands and fingers splayed across his chest, then shuddered when they travelled sensually down his sides to his thighs, feathering across the hair-roughened skin to enclose with startling intimacy his already quickening desire.

'Don't move,' she commanded huskily, and began to pleasure him, every action so instinctively known to her that she was more astonished than he, revelling in the way his flesh grew even further under her hands, thrilling to the knowledge that there was nothing she wouldn't do for him. Once he groaned and closed his eyes, his head tipping back in a gesture of sheer ecstasy.

Finally he put his drink down and took her hands in his, stilling her. She gazed at him, questioningly and adoringly.

'My turn, my darling,' he said thickly. 'My turn...'

CHAPTER NINE

SERINA swayed slightly as Aaron's words evoked a swamping wave of desire. He immediately took hold of her by the shoulders and turned her so that she was leaning against the cupboards for support.

'Not going to faint on me, are you?' he asked huskily.

She shook her head and shivered at the same time, though she wasn't aware of being cold.

His hands ran up and down her bare arms in a rubbing motion, then moved to the top button of her jacket.

Now her throat grew dry and she stiffened, an upsurge of nerves claiming her as she realised he just wanted her to stand there while he undressed her. It was no less than she had done to him, but somehow the reverse was more nerve-racking. She glanced agitatedly around the kitchen, suddenly aware of the bright fluorescent lights. Funny, she hadn't thought of them a moment ago when she'd been caressing Aaron so wantonly; had thought she was ready for anything!

She gulped as he reached the last button, her breathing coming hard and fast. Soon the button popped open and the jacket fell apart. Aaron's eyes darkened as he parted it further and pushed it back off her shoulders, whereupon it fell to the floor.

'You're so damned beautiful,' he rasped, his fingers moving over her slender shoulders, sliding down the satin straps of the black teddy, easing them down her arms. The lace moulding her full bust began to curl over and for a second was suspended from the hard tips of her breasts. But then it curled over again and she was naked to the waist.

She closed her eyes and held her breath, waiting for him to touch those rock-like peaks, *dying* for him to touch them.

He didn't. Instead, his hands went to the waistband of her skirt, undoing the button and sliding down the zip. The skirt pooled at her feet.

'And now,' he growled, sweeping one hand around her waist and one under her knees and lifting her to sit up on the marble counter. She sucked in a startled breath at the shock of the move and the cold of the marble, then gasped again when he parted her thighs and stood between them, the position bringing his mouth directly in line with her breasts. He leant forward and took one into his mouth, drawing the nipple and aureole deep into his hot, hungry cavern.

Serina couldn't help it. She cried out aloud, her back arching involuntarily with the sharply exquisite pleasure of it all. She clasped the edges of the counter with both hands and bit her bottom lip to stop any further sounds escaping.

After a while he deserted one breast in favour of the other, leaving the abandoned peak tingling and swollen. This he did time and time again till she had forgotten about trying to silence her moans. His hands began to help his onslaught, cupping each breast in turn, lifting and holding it to his avid lips and tongue.

He hasn't even kissed me yet, she thought dazedly, or touched me intimately, and yet I'm mad for him. I can feel it between my thighs and deep inside, hot and restless and yearning, aching to be filled and fulfilled.

'Aaron,' she groaned.

The pleading, tortured word told him all he needed to know, and he scooped her up around her buttocks and made his way to his bedroom.

Serina held her breath as he tipped her back on to the bed. The moment had come. He leant over her in the dimly lit room, unsnapping her teddy at the groin and stripping her naked, her black high heels the last to go.

'I want you naked too,' she rasped.

He laughed and threw away his robe, but he didn't take her straight away as she'd thought he would; instead he stretched out beside her and propped himself up on one elbow, his free hand running lightly over her breasts. She shivered uncontrollably, her lips parting with a gasp of sensuous pleasure every time his fingertips touched her nipples.

'How could any man resist you?' he said in a thickened voice and bent to cover her lips with his, to send his tongue to meet hers within her instantly eager mouth. Her left hand came to rest against his chest as he kissed her, and quite instinctively slid downwards, finding and caressing him again with tantalising fingers. A strangled groan of protest burst from his lungs and he grabbed her hand, then pinned both wrists above her head. 'Hell,' he gasped, looming over her. 'I should have brought handcuffs with me. What do you think I'm made of, woman?'

But she gave no verbal answer, her response to his question being to arch her body from the bed, to rub the tips of her breasts against his chest. He made a frustrated sound and moved to push her legs apart with his own, to lie between them.

Now, came the fevered frantic thought, now he would take her! Her knees lifted to accommodate him more easily, and for a brief, mad moment he surged against her oh, so willing flesh. But just as quickly he retreated. 'No...' His breathing was heavy and ragged. 'You won't catch me that easily, temptress mine. I've wanted you as I've wanted no other woman in my entire life... I've no intention of rushing this.'

And he held her prisoner with one hand while he rolled to one side and began to run his free hand over her body, first her breasts, then lower down, dipping into the hollow of her waist and belly, tracing her curves, and finally exploring those moist folds that encased the very centre of her need.

'No,' she moaned, the sensations too incredible. Her heartbeat trebled and there was an exquisite tension, a racing upwards as her muscles squeezed tighter and tighter. 'Oh, yes,' she decided with a gasp.

Quite abruptly Aaron abandoned her.

'Don't stop,' she groaned, struggling futilely against his hold.

'Patience, my sexy little siren... patience.' And he returned to caressing her breasts with light, feathery strokes, smothering any further verbal protests with his mouth.

Gradually she began to forget about that other elusive goal, the one that she had gone within a hair's breadth of winning. She sighed into his lips, her body almost relaxing beneath the gentle playing with her breasts, the softly sipping kisses.

Any relaxation was short-lived when his mouth left hers to start a slow wandering path down her body. She couldn't believe where he was heading, but heading there he was, and soon his lips and tongue were sending her into a wild frenzy as they tasted and tormented her with startling expertise. He knew just when to ease off, when to start again, how to keep her balancing on a knife-edge of agony and ecstasy. 'Aaron, please,' she pleaded, her head thrashing from side to side. 'No more...please...no more.'

Immediately he slid back up her body, holding himself above her as he wrapped her legs around his hips, her arms around his waist. His face was dark with passion, his breathing laboured as he hesitated that one last second. Then with a single forceful stroke he took her, his strangled cry piercing the silent room as he sank completely into her marvellously ready flesh.

Serina, however, was wide-eyed and speechless, so stunned was she by the experience, for as Aaron's body joined with hers she was engulfed by the most powerful wave of emotion. It rolled up through her stomach, her chest, her head, making her head spin, making her think of nothing but how much she loved this man, how she wanted nothing more than to remain one flesh with him forever. Her hands slid down the curve of his back to spread out across the hard, bunched muscles of his buttocks, her fingers tightening on his satiny flesh, pulling him in deeper and tighter.

He groaned and began thrusting, slowly at first, then more vigorously, his quickening tempo betraying a wild urgency that Serina empathised with. She too felt the need to move, to match his escalating rhythm. She did so, and within seconds that incredible tension was back, stronger than before and much more pleasurable. Electric currents charged along her nerve-endings, coiling her tighter and tighter till suddenly her breath caught and her muscles convulsed around him, blinding her with a series of explosive sensations that had no comparison.

'Oh, Aaron . . . Aaron,' she gasped as orgasm followed orgasm.

Though nothing, Serina decided later, could compare with the satisfaction she received when she felt Aaron's flooding release, heard his climactic cry. It was as though at that moment they were indeed one flesh, one being, one soul. She held him tight till his shudders subsided, not minding the feel of his weight when he collapsed down upon her.

Aaron must have interpreted her sigh differently, however, for suddenly he rolled over, taking her with him. His hands were firm on her hips, pressing and holding her close, keeping them joined while he settled her to lie across him, her head on his chest, her legs stretched along the bed on either side of him. She wanted to lift her head, to smile at him and tell him how wonderful he was, but somehow her head felt too heavy, and her tongue was thick in her throat.

'Go to sleep,' he husked, and began stroking her hair.

She sighed again and dragged her hands out from under his back, curling them lazily around his shoulders. An incredible weariness was sweeping over her, dragging at her limbs. A blackness clutched at the edges of her mind.

She must have slept for quite a while, for when she awoke her mind was quite clear and all traces of exhaustion were gone. She felt very alive, startlingly alive, and very, very aware of Aaron's hands feathering lightly up and down her spine. When they strayed further downwards she gasped.

'Rejoined the living, have you?' he whispered.

She lifted her head and shoulders and instantly became stunningly aware of something else. Aaron was fully aroused again, the feel of his hardness within her sending a hot jab of desire into her quickly stirring brain.

Slowly, ever so slowly, she sat upright, her knees pressing down on either side of him, holding his startled eyes with a decidedly seductive gaze. No other woman, she decided, could love a man as much as she loved this man. She would show him how much, she would make love to him as no other woman had loved him before.

'Aaron...' Slowly, she leant forward, letting the lush heaviness of her breasts rub sensuously over his chest. She smoothed back his ruffled hair with tantalising fingers, cupped his face, then kissed him, rocking slowly back and forth as she slid her tongue in and out of his mouth.

'Do you want me to continue?' she asked throatily when she withdrew to press her lips to his throat.

'Silly question,' he choked out.

Serina laughed seductively but sat upright, reaching up to remove the combs from her hair and throw them away. She shook her head so that the soft pale waves fell around her face, over her shoulders, some of the curls cascading down on to her breasts. Then she remained deliciously still, staring down at him with a sultry gaze, her chin lifting proudly, her full lips parting invitingly. She had not realised till that moment how natural the part of vamp came to her, yet she was relishing the role, loving the way she felt when she saw the flashes of desire blaze deep in Aaron's eyes.

His hands reached for her breasts again, but she merely laughed and slid them down on to her hips, leaning forward to kiss him again.

'I'm going to make mad passionate love to you,' she promised against his mouth. 'All you have to do is lie there and be still...' Her hands gripped his shoulders and her moist mouth trailed down to the base of his throat, kissing and licking his heated skin before moving further down his chest.

She felt his hands tighten around her hips, heard him expel a shuddering breath when she finally straightened and began to move with up and down slightly circular motions. Aaron groaned his satisfaction at her technique and her actions grew faster, more uninhibited, her internal muscles clenching him tighter and tighter till he could no longer lie still beneath her. His body arched upwards again and again. He grasped her waist, moving her violently above him, rocketing her to a bitter-sweet climax with devastating speed. Only then, it seemed, did he let himself go, his explosive release extending her pleasure for a few delicious seconds before once again that draining languor took over, making her slump across him in utter exhaustion.

He held her to him and stroked her back while she lay across him, both their breathing laboured, their hearts still pounding in their chests.

'You're fantastic in bed, do you know that?' he said at last. 'The best.'

Serina tried not to feel any hurt. But there was still a little niggle of dismay. For her it had been the ultimate experience, making love to the man she loved; the only man she had ever loved. Her sentimental soul wanted Aaron to say warm, sweet, loving things to her, not give a rating of her sexual performance.

But you knew what you were doing, the voice of honesty piped up. Don't be so damned stupid.

She sighed and snuggled closer.

'Tired?' Aaron asked softly.

'Mmm.'

'Cold?'

'Not really.'

"You will be soon. Come on, let's get into bed properly.'

She moaned when he slid out from under her, hating his body leaving hers. He climbed out and yanked back the bedding, rolling her between the sheets before slipping in beside her. But she sighed her contentment when he drew her close again, kissing her before turning her over and cuddling round her in spoon fashion, his hands cupping her breasts, one of his legs wedged between hers.

'Do you realise we haven't had any dinner?' he said.

'I'm not hungry any more,' she murmured dreamily.

He laughed. 'Neither am I . . . or at least . . .' he nuzzled her ear '. . . not for a while . . .' One hand came up to tip her head back over her shoulder, sipping at her slightly swollen mouth with the softest of kisses. 'Go to sleep, my darling . . . go to sleep.'

Serina's heart turned over. Darling . . . He called her darling . . . Dared she hope?

But there were no more thoughts for Serina that night, sleep snatching her mind from consciousness, sending her into a black tunnel where everything was quiet and warm and safe. She slept on and on, without a single dream or unhappy thought to disturb her peace.

CHAPTER TEN

SERINA gradually surfaced from sleep into that twilight world of semi-consciousness. She stirred slightly, pulling the sheet up around her neck and burrowing her face into the pillow. Her eyes remained blissfully shut. Never had she felt so lazy. Never had her bed seemed so comfortable.

'Breakfast, m'lady,' came the surprising announcement.

Serina's eyes did not fly open straight away but her mind jolted to instant awareness. It *wasn't* her bed. It *wasn't* her room. It was Aaron's.

Aaron...

A delicious wave of pleasure rippled through her as she recalled their incredible lovemaking. Never could Serina have envisaged anything as marvellous. *Surely* Aaron had to feel something deeper than just lust? He'd been so very loving towards her afterwards, had called her darling with real feeling. To cynically believe he was just using her was unacceptable.

Besides, how could she give up on her dream now? Or even regret having made love with the man she loved? Hadn't he brought out the real woman in her, shown her she could be as passionate and uninhibited as the next person? She liked her sexually awakened self, liked knowing she only had to touch him, kiss him, and he would want her.

Just thinking about it sent her heart thudding wildly in her chest. She opened her lashes slowly, a sensual

and inviting smile on her lips as she hoisted herself
up in the bed and pushed her hair back out of her
eyes.

Aaron was standing next to the bed, dressed for
work, a tray in his arms. His eyes were oddly unreadable as they flicked over her bare breasts, the
muscles in his jaw clenching when he turned to lower
the tray to the bedside chest, pushing the clock and
lamp backwards to make room.

'Orange juice, bacon and eggs, two slices of
wholemeal toast and coffee... and good morning,'
he finished, bending forward to give her a very pla-
tonic kiss on her forehead.

Serina couldn't resist trying out her newly dis-
covered power.

'And good morning to you, too,' she murmured,
her hands snaking up to curve around his neck, pulling
him down on to her mouth before he could straighten.
For a second he resisted, but then his lips parted with
a groan, and he sank to the bed, quickly taking control
in a long, thorough kiss. His hands slid up and down
her naked spine then pressed her breathtakingly close,
her breasts flattening against his suit jacket.

His eyes were dark and glittering by the time he
released her.

'You make a very sexy butler,' she said thickly.

But when she went to lean back into the embrace
he stood up.

'We aim to please,' he said crisply. 'Besides, the
least I could do was feed you after making you miss
dinner last night.' His glance at the clock was accom-
panied by a swift frown. 'Look, I hate to kiss and
run but I have to go. Craig leaves on his holidays this
morning and I promised to meet him at the office at

nine. I'll ring you later and let you know what's going on, whether I can get off early or not.'

His obvious eagerness to leave her brought an instant dismay. It was only seven-thirty. My God, how long did he think it took to drive to north Sydney from here? Certainly not one and a half hours.

Didn't he feel the way she did? Was his passion for her already sated? He had certainly just kissed her back with enthusiasm. Yet now he seemed anxious to get out of her sight. 'Oh...all right,' she mumbled. A stab of hurt at this sudden turn-around had her clutching at the sheet and dragging it up over her breasts. Bleak blue eyes dropped to the bed.

He sighed. 'Please don't be like that, Serina. It's not that I want to go. I *have* to.'

'Do you?' she asked, her eyes slowly lifting, her chin trembling, her heart sinking into a black abyss. 'Are you sure you really want me here when you get back, Aaron? Are you *sure*?'

The flash of doubt she saw chilled her to the bone. 'You want to leave it at a one-night stand, don't you?' she accused in a low, despairing voice.

'No, of course I don't,' he said irritably. 'I just don't want...' He broke off and sighed in obvious frustration.

'You don't want *what*?' she urged in desperation.

He grimaced. 'The thing is, when I woke up and found you in bed with me I...I didn't realise how it would feel.'

'How it would feel? I don't understand. What do you mean?'

'Damn it all, Serina, use your imagination! There you were, naked and luscious. I wanted you again. No, I *needed* you again. Madly. Uncontrollably. I had to get out of bed and take a long, cold shower.'

'But . . . *why*? Why didn't you wake me? I wouldn't have turned you down.'

'Don't you think I know that?' he flared. 'That's part of the problem, your . . . sensuality, your . . . expertise. It's rather addictive. Look, I said I needed you but I don't want to need you like that.' A sudden black anger swept over his face. 'I don't want to need *anyone* like that!'

She stared at him, appalled and desolate. It had all backfired on her. Everything. She'd have been far better off doing what she had always done, just lying there like a log. 'If you want me to go,' she said brokenly, 'then just say so. My God, at least be honest!'

His eyes widened then narrowed as he glared at her. 'Honest?' His face became even blacker. '*Honest?*' he repeated, his rapidly growing fury astonishing her. 'Since when have I been anything but honest with you? I didn't exactly *force* you into my bed last night, Serina. You came willingly enough, without any avowals of love, without any promises of undying devotion. Honest!' His top lip curled up with derision. 'That's a word you women should take to heart!

'And before you start defending yourself,' he went on savagely, 'look at your behaviour a moment ago. When I said I had to go to work, you looked offended, hurt even, as if I were a groom deserting his bride after their wedding night. Sure, that increased my doubts about having you stay till the end of the week, because the Serina I asked to stay didn't seem the type of girl who would sulk to try to get her own way, who would act the role of possessive lover. I don't need that sort of manipulative behaviour in my life. Not only do I not need it but I have no intention of putting up with it!' He glared down at her, his eyes hard and merciless. 'So if that's how you want to play the game then perhaps you *had* better leave!'

She blinked up at him, her mind racing. Good God, what sort of woman must his wife have been to have left wounds like this? Worse...could the wounds ever be healed? Serina doubted it, but she loved him too much to throw him to the wolves by running away. His admission of having wanted her so much propped up what was left of her crumbling hopes.

You could be wrong, Aaron, she thought as she looked at his coldly cynical face. Perhaps you do need to need someone like that. You need to be wrenched out of this void you've been existing in for too long and made to feel again, even if only sexually at first. So I'm going to hang in here and be the woman you want me to be, and if that means playing the free and easy spirit for you then I'll do that too, and one day you're going to wake up and find I've become a part of your life and you're never going to want to let me go.

'I'm sorry, Aaron,' she said with feeling. 'Of course you have to go to work, but please, try to understand...last night was so wonderful, so...special that I was upset when I thought you didn't want me any more, that you wanted me to leave. Forgive me?' She lifted pleading eyes, her smile warm and apologetic.

For a second she thought he wasn't going to give in. Then suddenly he made an impatient sound and sat down, literally dragging her into his arms. His kiss was hard and hungry, and by the time he pushed her back to arm's length his eyes were glittering with undeniable passion. 'Do you still think I want you to leave?'

'No,' she said shakily.

'I want you, Serina,' he insisted, 'and I want to be with you. But I must lay down some ground rules in case you haven't understood...'

'Yes?'

'Don't fall in love with me. Don't expect me to ever marry you. I'm not interested. I'm free now and I want to stay that way. I don't want to have to answer to anyone but Aaron Kingsley for a long, long while. If you can't accept that then perhaps it would be better if we called it quits right now!'

'I see,' she murmured, and looked down. Her heart was hammering against her ribs, for this was her first test, and a cruel one it was—to hear the man she loved verbally rip her dreams to shreds but to keep on understanding and hoping and fighting for him.

She lifted amazingly steady eyes to his, a sexy smile coming to her lips. 'Well... now that we've got that all settled why don't we kiss and make up?'

He stared at her for several seconds then crushed her to him, ravaging her lips with a starved hunger that took her breath away. 'I've never known anyone like you,' he rasped, his cheek rubbing against hers. 'You're incredible... you're...'

She cupped his face and brought his mouth back to hers, loving him with her lips, her tongue, her whole being.

'God, but I must have you,' he groaned, reefing away and stripping off his jacket, then tugging madly at his tie.

She knelt up on the bed and helped him with the buttons on his shirt. 'But won't you be late?' she asked, worried that he might think she had deliberately tried to seduce him.

'It's not that late.' He ripped off his shirt and started on the belt of his trousers.

Serina stared at him, stunned not only by his passion but her own. She helped him drag his clothes down, and before he could say a word bent to take him between her lips. He gasped, his hands shaking uncontrollably as they reached to splay into her hair.

Aaron rang her shortly after eleven-thirty to say that unfortunately he couldn't get home for lunch as he'd hoped.

'I have to take a client out for a Christmas drink and dinner,' he explained. 'Craig made the arrangement before he realised he would be leaving early today, so it's up to me to step in.'

'Can't be helped,' she said blithely.

He was silent for a second. 'Well, what have you been doing since I staggered out the door a couple of hours ago?'

She laughed. 'I'm afraid I didn't eat your delicious breakfast. It was cold by the time I got to it. I drank the orange juice, though, then had a shower and went back to bed for a snooze.'

'Lucky you.'

'Now I'm about to make some fresh toast and coffee, after which I'm going to read. I see you have a large selection of bestsellers in the bookcase next to this phone.'

'And what do you fancy out of them? I won't try to guess, lest I tread on another of your toes.'

'I haven't made up my mind yet.'

'Do you like thrillers?'

'I like just about anything.'

'Mmm. Tell me more,' he drawled in a low, sexy voice. 'Oh, damn, there's a call on the other line. Must go, Serina. See you as soon as I can. Probably around four.'

He hung up, and Serina danced off to the kitchen. Everything was going quite well. He had rung her as he had promised, and had sounded really happy.

You're going to be so happy with me, Aaron Kingsley, she vowed. So happy. Just you wait and see!

Serina was still in the kitchen, wearing Aaron's bathrobe and making herself her second cup of coffee, when she heard the rattle of a key in the front door. Her eyes darted to the wall clock. Twelve sixteen. Aaron must have got out of the lunch-date. Her heart somersaulted with instant excitement and she dashed into the living-room just in time to see Craig closing the front door behind him.

Her gasp of shock had his head jerking round, his eyes taking her in, first with astonishment and then with a knowing understanding. 'Well, well, so Aaron ran into a traffic snarl this morning, did he?' His chuckle was lewd and knowing. 'He might have told me, the lucky devil.' Craig's narrowed gaze settled on her bare feet then moved upwards in a slow scrutiny. 'Yes, indeed,' he muttered, 'as I've said to him, a very lucky devil...'

Serina's hands fluttered up to hold the robe defensively closed around her right up to her neck. 'You're supposed to have left on your holidays.' Her shaking voice showed her agitation at being alone with this man. Casually dressed in jeans and black T-shirt, Aaron's business partner looked much more rugged and infinitely more powerful than he had the night she'd first met him. He cocked a single eyebrow at her then turned and locked the door behind him.

'What...what do you think you're doing?' Serina choked out, fear tightening her throat and chest.

He whirled back to give her a surprised look. 'Doing? I'm going to get my favourite beach hat. I left it here a couple of weekends ago.'

She backed away as he began to walk towards her. 'But...but you locked the door! Why did you lock the door?'

He stopped and frowned, glancing back over his shoulder. 'Oh, that.' He shrugged. 'Habit, I suppose. I lived here for a while when I was getting my divorce, and Aaron always insisted on it. You must know what he's like.' His eyes turned back to stare at her panic-stricken face. Suddenly he shook his head, his expression exasperated. 'For God's sake, Serina, don't be such a little ninny. I might not be a saint but I draw the line at forcing myself on my best mate's lady. Hell, give me credit for some morals!'

Her obvious relief made his frown darken further. 'You know, sweetheart, I think you might be a fraction paranoiac. I mean, OK, so I gave you the once-over, but hell, you're going to be looked at, woman! You're not only well stacked, you're bloody beautiful and sexy as all hell. You can't expect the whole male race to go around with their eyes shut.'

His blunt honesty took her by complete surprise, and she had to concede that she had become rather defensive over the years. Maybe she had over-reacted. Maybe...

He sighed and brushed past her to stride into the kitchen, where he rattled around in the broom cupboard. She wandered across to stand nervously in the doorway. 'Not in here,' he muttered. 'You wouldn't have seen a large straw hat, would you? Mexican-style, with pompoms hanging off it?'

'Sorry.' The mind boggled at this man wearing such a hat, anyway.

'Damn! How can I go to Fiji without my favourite hat?'

'It might be in the bedroom,' she suggested. 'Shall I look for you?'

'Nope...I'll do it. I know the layout.' And he strode into the bedroom with Serina trailing behind at a safe distance. Wardrobe doors were flung open, but no hat.

'Why don't you call Aaron at the office?' she tried. 'He might know where it is.'

'No point. He won't be there by now. He had an appointment in the city at twelve-thirty. You know Aaron. He's never late. Or not usually,' he added, with a dry glance at the still rumpled bed.

Serina's face flushed with colour.

'The linen press!' Craig exclaimed and stalked out of the bedroom and into the main bathroom. 'Aah, here it is,' he called out, emerging with the hat on his head. Serina gaped at the ridiculous sight.

Craig grinned. 'Keeps the flies off,' he said, and waggled his head. The pompoms swung madly to and fro. 'I think your kettle's boiling,' he added.

Serina scuttled off to the kitchen, with Craig hot on her heels. 'You wouldn't have a cup of coffee for me, would you? I've been on the go since breakfast.'

Serina was still not entirely comfortable at being alone with Craig with only a bathrobe on, but she could hardly refuse. And he *had* proved that he wasn't quite the lecher she had first thought him.

'So!' he exclaimed once he'd settled himself on a stood with his mug of coffee in front of him. 'You and Aaron been an item for long?'

'An item?' she repeated.

He shrugged. 'Sleeping together, then.'

She glared at him across the kitchen counter. 'Is that any of your business?'

He pulled a face. 'Maybe. Maybe not. I guess anything that could make Aaron happy or unhappy is my business. Poor bastard deserves a break. I've been telling him for ages that what he needs is a sexy, co-operative blonde in his life instead of the odd one-night stand, but I certainly wouldn't like to see some gold-digging little bimbo try to play him for a sucker.'

Craig's verbal broadside was delivered with such indifference to her feelings that Serina was more shocked than insulted at first. But the heat was not long in coming to her face, her temper rising quickly. 'My God, who you think you are, saying that to me? Bimbo indeed! It's *me* who'll end up getting hurt, stupid, co-operative blonde *me*, who's giving him what he needs even though he's told me quite clearly that I can expect nothing back. Does that sound as if I'm a...a *gold-digger*?' Tears of anger and hurt flooded into her eyes.

Craig's mouth had dropped open. 'Good grief, you're really in love with him, aren't you?'

'And what if I am?' she threw back at him. 'Obviously you don't think I'm good enough for your precious friend anyway, so what difference does it make?'

'Serina...I didn't mean...I...'

She dashed the tears away with the backs of her hands. 'Just drink your rotten coffee and get out of here, will you?' she pronounced, and stormed from the kitchen, marching into the bedroom and slamming the door behind her.

She leant against the door, chest heaving, hating herself for having lost her cool, but hating Craig even more. The man was a snobbish, insensitive clod!

The knock on the bedroom door was tentative. 'Serina? Look, I'm sorry, love. Truly, I wasn't referring to you specifically, though you've got to realise how you come across sometimes. I mean, you've been around, love, living here, living there, working at all sorts of things. And Aaron is one hell of a catch. Look, it's great that you really love him, but for God's sake don't tell him you do or he'll have a blue fit. Damn, but you've got yourself into a sticky situation here. There's a lot you should know about the guy or you really *will* get hurt. Badly. Come on out, love, and sit with me for a while. I think I should tell you about Aaron's marriage so you'll at least be forewarned . . .'

How could she resist the opportunity to know more about the man she loved, to have some more pieces of the puzzle of his past slotted into place? Serina had no option but to wipe her eyes and come out, though her whole body was tense, her head pounding with the beginnings of a splitting headache. Craig put a comforting arm around her shoulder and drew her over to settle her on one of the kitchen stools. Then he walked round and topped up both their coffees with boiling water.

'Where to begin?' he mused as he slid her mug over to her. 'At the beginning, I suppose, when I first met Aaron. It was at college, not long after he was married to Naomi. We were both doing a part-time course in business at Kuring-gai campus. Aaron was busy with his Iron Man feats, I was working days at an accountancy company as a clerk. Maybe we were drawn to each other because I too had married young, though not for the same reasons as Aaron. One eventually got the impression that, if it hadn't been for Christine, there wouldn't have been a marriage. Not that he didn't appear to love Naomi. What not to love? She was a gorgeous-looking bird and devoted to him. Too devoted, as it turned out.'

'So I gathered,' Serina put in. 'Jillian said she was neurotically jealous, even suggesting that Naomi sent Christine to boarding-school to get her out of the way, though that does seem a bit extreme.'

'You'd better believe it. That's exactly the sort of thing she would do. Aaron wanted more children but she refused. Couldn't bear the thought of sharing him further.'

'I'm surprised the marriage lasted,' Serina said thoughtfully.

'So am I, quite frankly, especially after he was injured and had to give up competitive surfing.'

'He was injured?'

'Broke his leg in two places. It didn't knit properly for a long time. Oh, but Naomi liked that, liked his having to give up what he loved. She hated Aaron being out of her sight, hated his having other interests, hated his having friends. She particularly hated me; thought I was a bad influence on him, especially when we went into business together and then I upped and got a divorce. Now that really put a cat among the pigeons! She started ringing the office several times a day, checking where Aaron was. If he was a minute late getting home, or meeting her somewhere, they would have the most frightful row. Once when he had a minor car accident and was half an hour late getting home she'd called the police in.'

'I see...' Her heart turned over as she thought of his obsession with punctuality. And it was no wonder he didn't want to have to answer to anyone for a while. 'Still,' she said aloud, 'I find it hard to believe Aaron put up with that. He's a very strong-willed man.'

'Don't get me wrong. He fought her tooth and nail sometimes, but the child was always his undoing. Naomi used his love for Christine to hold him. Little did she know that even that ploy finally ran out of steam. He was going to leave her and fight for custody of Christine.'

'But . . . but he didn't, did he?'

'No. . .' A black cloud passed over Craig's face. 'The very day he told me what he was going to do he got a call from Naomi's doctor, telling him that he was to come home, that his wife had collapsed with terminal cancer and had only weeks to live at best. What could he do? Desert her in her hour of need? Besides, in one way—horrible though it was—his problem had resolved itself.'

Serina shuddered. 'How ghastly!'

'You haven't heard the worst of it. Do you know what the doctor told Aaron—what Naomi told him later too? She could have been saved. She'd had these lumps in her breasts for ages but refused to do anything about them, thought Aaron wouldn't desire her any more if she'd had to have them removed, or if she lost her hair through chemotherapy. She told Aaron quite calmly that a couple of years' extra being beautiful for him, having him make love to her was worth dying for, that she would do the same thing again.'

'Oh, God. . .the poor, sick woman. . . Poor *Aaron*!'

'He was devastated. But he pulled himself together and did everything he could to make Naomi's dying as peaceful and happy as possible. He pretended as he'd never pretended before, but it took an enormous toll on him emotionally. I thought after Naomi's death he would snap out of it, but instead he became hard and cynical where women were concerned. A taker.

Which is what worries me with you, Serina. You're not the first woman he's had since his wife's death, believe me. Though you're the first he's kept for more than one night. Be careful. It doesn't mean he loves you.'

Serina sat staring silently into her coffee. Aaron had been tempted to throw her out after one night ... But he hadn't. Why hadn't he? Was it just that he'd decided a mistress was more convenient and safer than casual sex? Or could he possibly care about her more than he liked to admit?

Dear me, but it was all more complicated than she'd imagined. That wife of his had been very sick, very destructive. Could the pieces she had left behind ever be put together? Thank the lord she *had* sent Christine to boarding-school. It had got the child out of that unhealthy situation.

Craig reached over and gently covered her hand with his. 'I'd like to tell you he might fall in love with you. But I don't think he will. It's too soon. Far too soon. Even if he did, he certainly wouldn't marry you. So, if you're looking for wedding bells and baby booties, then forget it. The man couldn't cope.'

The sound of another key rattling in the front-door lock startled both of them, and they stared, wide-eyed and speechless, as Aaron came in and shut the door. But there was nothing wide-eyed and speechless about Aaron as he walked slowly towards them, particularly when his eyes spotted the way Craig's hand was still covering Serina's.

CHAPTER ELEVEN

'A DETOUR on your way to the airport, Craig?' came his coldly cutting comment.

Serina held her breath as Aaron's partner casually withdrew his hand and tipped up the rim of the ridiculous Mexican hat. 'Something like that, old man. You didn't expect me to go to Fiji without old faithful, did you? Sun-baking without a hat can be dangerous, you know.'

'There are more dangerous pursuits,' came the dark warning.

'True.' Craig managed a laugh but Serina could see he was not at ease. Aaron was looking thunderous, and there was an ominous quality about the way he kept flipping his keys from one hand to the other. She might have felt somewhat hopeful because of his obvious jealousy if he weren't darting murderous glances her way as well.

'Thanks for the coffee, Serina,' Craig tossed off with clearly feigned nonchalance. 'See you, Aaron.' He began making for the front door then stopped. 'Oh, by the way, what happened to your lunch with Pete? Didn't he turn up?'

'He left a message at the restaurant that he couldn't make it.'

'Aah . . . I thought it had to be something like that. Well, *arrivederci! Au revoir! Adios!* See you in three weeks!' He whipped open the door and was gone.

Once the echo of the door's banging had died away the silence was electric. Serina could feel her stomach churning, not knowing how to tackle the situation, whether to explain Craig's presence further or just ignore Aaron's black humour. What would a free spirit do?

'You two looked cosy together,' he said at last, his words clipped and hard. He walked over and threw his keys on the counter next to her, then picked up Craig's coffee-mug. He stared into it for a second then strode over to pour the dregs down the sink. 'One could easily have thought I'd walked in on a rather intimate tête-à-tête . . .'

When she said nothing in her defence he whirled to face her, his eyes blazing. 'Well? Aren't you going to say something? Or do you think I'm stupid enough to believe it was all as innocent as you're pretending?' He walked slowly back and gripped the edge of the counter with wide-spread arms, leaning forward and glaring down at her, fury in every pore of his stiffly held body. 'I wouldn't be surprised if Craig had no idea you were setting him up for the kill, after you whetted his appetite the other night at dinner with your rebuff.'

She could not hide her shock, staring at him with wide eyes.

'That is your *modus operandi*, isn't it?' he scorned. 'Playing hard to get, letting the poor bloke think you don't want to have anything to do with him, then suddenly coming on so hot and strong that he goes off his head with wanting you!'

Serina was stunned by the accusation *and* Aaron's volatility. She had glimpsed his temper before, but he was actually shaking with the effort of containing his rage.

'Aaron,' she said with far more composure than she was feeling, '*nothing* happened between Craig and myself. He came here for his sun-hat, as he said, then stayed for a cup of coffee.'

The steely blue eyes narrowed dangerously, the muscle in his jaw twitching. 'And he needed to hold your hand to do that? God, Serina!' He whirled away and strode into the living-room. 'Do you take me for a bloody idiot?' he threw back at her. 'The truth is that if I hadn't come in when I did, you two would now be in there...' He waved his hand in the direction of the bedroom. 'Screwing away like mad!'

Her mouth dropped open. Then it snapped shut, her patience with him disintegrating in the face of such blind jealousy, such vile nastiness. 'That's enough, Aaron!' she bit out, rising to her feet, her blue eyes flashing angrily. 'You have absolutely no reason to believe any such thing. No reason at all. If you must know, Craig and I happened to be talking about *you* when you came in. He was telling me about your marriage, warning me that you carried scars, that...

'Oh, this is ridiculous,' she snapped, seeing the scepticism in those hard blue eyes, knowing in that split second that, despite loving Aaron, she could not bear to stay with him. She could not endure irrationality, could not stand a person's stubbornly believing something bad about her that wasn't true. 'I don't have to justify myself to you, Aaron,' she said brokenly. 'You want to be free? Then *be* free! All by yourself!' With this she lifted her quavering chin and marched past him into the bedroom.

She went to slam the door behind her but he was there, kicking it back open, coming into the room with savage intent. He grabbed her and swung her round to face him. 'I won't let you leave, Serina!'

'Won't you?' she flung up at him. 'And how do you propose to stop me? Beating me? Tying me up?

Do you think that would work, that I would meekly accept such behaviour? I would have thought that you, of all people, would understand how others react to a sick, jealous mind, Aaron. All they want to do is get as far away as they can, as quickly as they can.'

She saw the horror of what he was doing dawn in his eyes. He looked so appalled, so shattered that compassion swept through her, melting away her anger, bringing tears of sad understanding. But along with the tears came the resolution to lay some ground rules of her own. She stepped back from him and slowly unwrapped the towelling robe, letting it drop from her shoulders to pool at her feet. She stood before him, totally nude, her insides shaking.

'See these breasts, Aaron?' she cried, lifting their generous curves in her hands. 'They're *yours*! See this body?' She came forward and pressed her satiny skin against him. 'It's *yours*,' she husked, desperate blue eyes lifting to his. 'Not Craig's,' she choked out. 'Not any other man's. Last night was very special to me, Aaron. Very special... Believe me when I say I want nothing more than to keep on having nights like that. But I won't take what you've just dished out to me. I'll walk out first. I want to be free too, Aaron. Free of all the misconceptions men have of me, free of——'

He stopped her then, covering her trembling mouth with fevered lips and gathering her into a fierce embrace. 'I'm sorry,' he groaned, lifting his mouth to kiss the tears from her cheeks, her eyes. 'Sorry...' He clasped her so tightly that all the breath was slowly being squeezed out of her body. 'Forgive me... I won't ever do anything like that again.' he vowed huskily. 'Ever! I must have been mad! Hell, I do know how destructive jealousy is, believe me.' He pulled back then and held her face in strong hands. His kisses became sweet, gentle, heart-wrenchingly apologetic. 'Forgive me...'

It was testimony to Serina's love that she forgave him so quickly. More than forgave. With startling speed her only wish was that he make love to her, her rapidly ignited body sending a moaning, whimpering sound to her lips.

Aaron groaned his own desire and his kisses quickly resumed their previous ardour. 'I need you, Serina,' he muttered against her mouth. 'Now...quickly...'

She made no protest as his shaking hands laid her back across the end of the bed, watching with wide eyes and dry mouth as he voided himself of his clothes in a mad frenzy. There was no foreplay, nothing. She flowered open then closed over the titanic throbbing of his flesh, grasping his body close and deep, moving in time with his wild frantic rhythm till they were both crying out, both shuddering and clinging to each other.

'God,' he sighed, when at last they lay quietly beside each other. Then he laughed and rolled over to kiss her lightly and smile into her startled eyes. 'It's all your fault, you know, being so damned sexy. I want you so much all the time that I think all other men must be feeling the same.' He lifted a hand to trace her mouth with a single fingertip. 'You have forgiven me, haven't you?'

'I shouldn't,' she murmured, knowing in her heart that this was so, that loving this man was not going to work out for her. But, dear heaven, it was hard to think straight when she was in his arms, with the memory of what they had just shared still pulsating along her veins.

'I'll make it up to you,' he whispered seductively.

'Oh?' she murmured, her lips tingling under his feather-light touch. 'How?'

'By giving you whatever you like, whenever you like, as often as you like...' His hands drifted down to start lazily encircling one nipple after the other.

'Promises, promises,' she said carelessly, but her body was continuing to betray her. Already it burnt with the excitement his words and fingers were evoking.

He pretended to look offended. 'You doubt me?'

'Well...you did say that day on the beach that you weren't as fit as you should be, that you needed to work out a lot more.'

He chuckled. 'Want to put me to the test?'

She pouted her generous lips. 'I don't believe in setting myself up for disappointment.'

A decidedly wicked gleam blazed deep in his eyes. 'Then you don't know me very well, Serina, my love. I *always* rise to a challenge.'

Aaron had to go into the office the next day but he closed it up early, returning home by noon, where they took up where they'd left off the previous evening, making love again and again, punctuating their lengthy lovemaking sessions with long hot showers, lazy walks or a refreshing snack. Serina was past worrying about the possibilities, or the probabilities, of the future. She was so madly, so deeply in love with Aaron that to even contemplate life without him sent her into a mental whirl.

She gave herself up totally to his wishes, hoping against hope that her love would win out in the end. It certainly seemed to be working, for occasionally she surprised a look on his face that carried such warmth and affection that she believed it was only a matter of time before he wouldn't be able to live without her as well.

Aaron didn't want to take her home on the Saturday, wanting her to stay another day and night with him, but, since he had asked her to spend Christmas Day on the Sunday with him and Christine at Jillian's, Serina insisted on being taken home.

'I have to buy some presents,' she'd told him. 'And I'm in need of some fresh clothes. I can't spend my whole life either naked or in the one black suit.'

'Oh, I don't know,' he had drawled, that familiar gleam coming into his eyes again. They might have made love one more mad time if they hadn't had at that moment been speeding along the motorway. Though Serina suspected that if she had been willing Aaron might have ignored the no-stopping rule and pulled over to do just that. He couldn't seem to get enough of her, his passion awe-inspiring at times.

When they finally pulled up outside her house, she practically had to browbeat him not to accompany her inside.

'You promised to go home and help Christine decorate the tree,' was her winning argument. At last he reluctantly went on his way, but only after he had extracted *her* promise to be on Jillian's doorstep no later than eleven in the morning. She had refused to let him come all the way over to pick her up, saying she had her bike, and he should be able to enjoy a few glasses of Christmas cheer without having to worry about driving her home.

A decision she almost regretted when she awoke to a rainy Christmas morning, though luckily the showers held off for her ride over. She arrived shortly after eleven, looking like Santa Claus dressed in white jeans and a red and white striped top, with a red plastic shopping-bag full of presents.

Christine dashed down to the kerb to meet her. 'I heard the bike coming up the hill,' she explained brightly, turning to smile at her father who was following down the steep front path at a more sedate speed. 'Serina looks terrific, doesn't she, Dad?'

He looked pretty good himself, Serina thought, her eyes admiring his well-proportioned body in the smart blue jeans and pale blue shirt. For a second she stared at him, her mind stripping him of his clothes, recalling far too vividly how he looked kneeling over her on the bed, aroused and demanding. There was little of this cool, almost aloof-looking man when he was making love to her. Then he was all hot words and wild imagination, his demands both surprising and exciting her to make equally wild demands.

'Hmm, what on earth are you thinking?' he whispered as he bent to kiss her. 'Happy Christmas, Serina,' he added more loudly. 'And what did Santa bring me?' he teased and tried to peek into the red bag.

She smacked his hand. 'None of that,' she reprimanded. 'Presents can only be given out from under the tree.'

'Aah,' he grinned. 'A traditionalist.'

'Lucky you, Dad.' Christine laughed at a puzzled Serina. 'He's spent all morning putting up mistletoe everywhere, and I don't think it's to kiss me under!'

They all laughed, the moment heralding what proved to be a wonderful Christmas, even the overcast weather being to their advantage since it made the hot turkey dinner taste even better. Jillian seemed very pleased to have Serina for the day, but Serina suspected that Aaron's sister had no idea that she and her brother were already lovers. Aaron was reasonably careful not to be too familiar with her, though some of the glances he slipped her when the others weren't looking were definitely X-rated.

Serina mischievously made them all wait till after lunch to get their presents, saying that by the look of the discarded wrapping paper around the room they had already received enough presents for a while. Finally, though, the moment came when she played Santa and handed out the gaily wrapped gifts.

'A Ken Done bikini!' Christine squealed when she opened hers. 'And a matching shirt! Oh, Serina, I love them!' she cried, and gave her a kiss and a hug.

The elegant cream lace table-cloth for Jillian was just as big a hit, *and* the smart New Year's leather diary for Gerald.

Serina became a little nervous when Aaron took ages opening his present. Would he like it? she worried. Men *were* hard to buy things for.

Finally the ribbon and paper were off and Aaron stared down at the pale blue suede glasses-case, the Italian brand name in gold letters across one corner. Aaron's eyes lifted to hers, startled. 'Serina...thank you...but you shouldn't have, you know,' he reproached.

Oh, dear...she should have known he would recognise the exclusive and expensive brand. She hoped he didn't think she were trying to buy his love.

'Sunglasses!' Christine announced gaily as her father slowly drew them out of the case. 'Put them on, put them on.' He did as she asked and they all stared at him, the sleek wrap-around frames giving him an even sexier movie-star appeal. 'Wow! Tom Cruise, eat your heart out!' Christine enthused. 'Gosh, Dad, if you wear those sunglasses to the beach and sling the towel I gave you over your shoulders you'll have the women falling at your feet. You'd better not go with him, Serina. You'll be jealous.'

Aaron laughed and removed the sunglasses, popping them back into the case. 'Not Serina. She's not the jealous type.' His eyes found hers and she saw how pleased that thought made him. It reminded her forcibly that he was still suffering the after-effects of a long relationship with an almost neurotically possessive woman. Play it slow and cool, Serina. Slow and cool...

'Now give Serina *her* present, Dad,' Christine pressed.

'Yes, Aaron,' Jillian joined in, 'where did you hide it?'

'But I didn't expect anything,' Serina protested. 'Just having me here for the day was enough.'

'Don't be silly,' Gerald boomed. 'Christmas is for giving gifts.'

Aaron stood up and went over to the tree, pulling a small package out from its hiding place in the branches. It was wrapped in silver paper with a pink rosette on top. 'We decided to buy you one decent thing rather than a lot of little things,' he explained softly. 'If you don't like it it can be exchanged.'

'She'll like it,' Jillian said, a smile lighting up her face, giving its rather austere lines a warmer, more gentle expression.

Serina felt ridiculously excited and pleased as she opened the present. The size of the box bespoke jewellery, but she certainly didn't expect anything as beautiful as what she encountered. It was a ring, a lovely pearl ring, the large lustrous pearl circled by diamonds and mounted on a rich gold band.

She blinked up at Aaron, unable to find the right words to say.

He smiled and stepped forward, bending to take the box from her nerveless fingers, pulling the ring from its velvet bed and slipping it on the third finger of her right hand. 'Well, at least it fits,' he drawled.

She stared down at her hand, her fingers still tingling with his brief touch. 'It . . . it's lovely,' she managed at last. 'But . . .'

'No buts,' Jillian laughed. 'Aaron said you must like pearls since you have some of your own.'

'But it's too expensive!'

'Oh, pooh!' Christine waved a dismissive hand. 'Dad can afford it. He's loaded. Besides, Uncle Gerald chipped in.'

'And I can afford it too,' Gerald grinned.

'See?' Aaron said, blue eyes amused. 'Of course, if you insist, we could take it back and exchange it for something more practical, like a toaster.'

She shot her hands under her arms. 'Just you try and prise it away from me!' she warned.

They all laughed at her.

'Well, now that that's over, anyone for a game of poker?' Gerald suggested. 'You can play, can't you, Serina?'

'Yes.'

'What about five hundred?' Jillian said. 'I don't like poker much.'

'I can play that too,' Serina confessed.

'Great!'

'Is there anything you can't do?' Aaron teased her as they were setting up the card-table. Gerald and Jillian were in the kitchen, getting drinks and peanuts. Christine had left to visit a girlfriend next door to show off her new bikini.

Serina pretended to give the matter serious thought. 'Rescue a drowning surfer?' she decided upon.

Aaron shook his head. 'I'll bet you could do that too. All you'd have to do is stand at the shore and wave his way and he'd recover in an instant.'

She gave him a reproving look.

'OK, I'm exaggerating,' he admitted, 'but promise me one thing: don't go giving mouth-to-mouth resuscitation to anyone!'

Her smile was decidedly sexy. 'Not even you?'

He groaned and went to reach for her when Gerald came back into the room.

'I'll get you later,' Aaron whispered under his breath.

But as it turned out there was no later that day for Aaron and Serina. By seven o'clock Serina wasn't feeling very well, an icky feeling in her stomach. She knew what it was—her period was due that day—but she kept this private and personal matter from her host and hostess and made some excuse about having to get home to take phone calls from her brothers.

To Aaron, though, she told the truth when he walked her to her bike, explaining that she was usually as sick as a dog for at least a day and he should leave her to her misery. To which he said what rot, that he was going to come over the next day and look after her.

Serina's first reaction was to refuse. She hated people fussing over her when she felt lousy, but Aaron finally convinced her that he really wanted to be with her, so she acquiesced, feeling pleased that he wanted her company even when they couldn't make love.

She climbed on to her scooter, smiling her satisfaction. 'But if you start holding my hand and making me cups of tea,' she warned, 'I'll send you packing. I can't stand that sort of thing.'

His face was puzzled. 'Then what am I supposed to do?'

'Bring a bottle of Jack Daniel's and a video,' she suggested. 'Distraction is the best medicine.'

'What video? I don't know what you've seen?'

'Take pot luck, but nothing too sexy.'

'Agreed.'

He leant forward then to give her a lingering kiss on the mouth. 'I hate to think of your being all alone in that house, feeling sick,' he said.

She shrugged. 'I'll survive.'

His lips pursed into a disgruntled expression. 'You really know how to make a guy feel needed!'

Her face must have shown that she found his attitude bewildering. She'd thought he liked her being independent.

He shook his head in obvious exasperation. 'I must be mad ... I should be glad you are as you are ... but sometimes I ...' An odd expression flitted across his face. For a second he looked lost, confused. 'Old habits die hard, I suppose,' he sighed. 'You'd better go. I'll see you tomorrow, after lunch.'

He didn't kiss her again.

Serina's period didn't arrive that night, despite her suffering from severe cramps. Several trips to the bathroom soon established that she was the victim of a gastric upset, perhaps from eating too many cashews and peanuts all afternoon. By the next morning she was feeling marginally better, though drained, but there was absolutely no sign of anything else, a fact that had her quite puzzled. For years one could have set a clock by her monthly cycle. Not that she was worried about pregnancy. This week had been a relatively safe time of the month for one thing, but she had still faithfully used the diaphragm the doctor had prescribed for her.

She came downstairs shortly after eleven and began making herself a light breakfast, trying to remember the last time she had been late by more than a few hours.

The answer was never, except once during her final school exams. Her mother had told her it was probably because of stress.

Serina sighed and frowned to herself over her vegemite toast and black coffee. Could this be a similar state of affairs? she wondered. Certainly, she had been under all sorts of stress lately, with her mother's death and problems with her brothers, and then Aaron's coming into her life. That had to be it, she decided. No doubt nature would get its wheels going again soon. It was nothing to worry about.

She bit lethargically into the toast, forcing her mind to other things, like what she would put on before Aaron arrived. But a tiny niggling doubt refused to go away. What if there was something really wrong with her?

CHAPTER TWELVE

AARON arrived shortly before two, bringing with him not only the bottle of whisky Serina had mentioned but the video of *Out of Africa*—which luckily she had never seen—and several choices of mixer drinks, some cold turkey and salad, courtesy of Jillian.

'She really likes you.' Aaron told her.

'Well, you don't have to look so surprised,' she smiled, having determined not to worry about the other matter. Serina was not one to brood. She had found over the years that most things one worried about never happened, so she had gradually adopted a philosophy not to worry till it was absolutely necessary. Her mother had been a worrier, as had her father. Perhaps that was why she had finally decided not to be.

'You don't look too bad,' Aaron said as she ushered him into the kitchen. His eyes flicked over the blue jeans and colourful shirt she had worn shopping with Christine. Her hair was secured back in a rubber band, her face devoid of make-up. 'A bit pale. Are you in pain? I brought some painkillers in case you didn't have any.'

His thoughtfulness pleased her but she shook her head at him and turned away to put the spare bottles of dry ginger ale in the fridge. 'I'm not feeling on top of the world but I'm coping. And the only painkiller I'm going to try is that,' she said, pointing to the bottle of Jack Daniel's. The years had also taught her that a couple of shots of whisky cured anything from a tension headache to toothache to stomach cramps.

'You're not a closet drunk, are you?' he teased.

'Only on certain days of the month.'

'And when can we hope to resume . . . relations?'

His directness rattled her and she didn't answer straight away, but turned to pull a tray of ice-cubes out of the freezer so that she could start mixing herself a drink. 'Want one?' she asked.

'Sure. But straight on the rocks. No ginger ale.'

She nodded and proceeded to pour the drinks, not deliberately ignoring his question but mulling over what she would say. There was no denying her dismay, for there she'd been, thinking he liked her company just as much without sex, that he must care about her more than he realised.

Her eyes slid over his impressively male body, housed to advantage in hip-hugging stone-washed jeans and snug white T-shirt, and that tight little feeling turned over in her stomach. It would have been so very easy to tell him she had been mistaken about the time of the month, that it had merely been a tummy bug, knowing that the afternoon would then end in their making love. But along with the physical desire lay another desire, the desire to see how Aaron would handle her company without sex. Besides, Mother Nature would probably remedy that other matter any second so it wasn't even a real lie.

'About New's Year Eve, I would think,' she said, giving him a slightly stiff smile as she handed over his drink.

He lifted it to his lips with a sigh. 'An eternity away.'

'No one's forcing you to spend your time with me,' she snapped. 'There are other women who I'm sure aren't similarly indisposed. Or do you expect me to service you some other way?'

Slowly he lowered the glass to the counter, his eyes hardening. 'You expect me to ask that of you, Serina?'

She shook her head and dropped her eyes to the floor. Yes, she thought desolately. Pretend outrage if you like, but *yes*, that's exactly what I think you came here hoping for. You're no different to the others. You never were. I was just a fool, believing what I wanted to believe, hoping against hope that, because you invited me to spend Christmas with your family and even gave me a ring, I meant more to you than just a means to an end.

Aaron's hand shot out to grab her chin and he forced her face up to look at him. 'I don't deserve that, Serina. I'm no saint, God knows, but I'm not that rotten and selfish.' He dropped her chin and drew her firmly into his arms. 'It's *you* who I want to be with, lovemaking or no, not some other woman.'

She made a small sobbing sound in her throat and laid her head against his chest. 'I thought...'

'Thought what?' He held her away and looked at her with exasperated eyes.

'I...I thought that all you wanted from me was just sex.'

'Now when did I ever say that, Serina? I recall I said that I wanted you to be my woman. That doesn't necessarily mean just in bed...I think I'm proving that right now.'

'Yes...yes, I suppose so.' She frowned, and rubbed a shaky hand across her forehead.

'Don't frown, my lovely.' He bent to kiss her forehead softly, sweetly. 'Listen, I've been thinking... It looks as if I'll be able to move into this house in a couple of weeks. My solicitor is doing a rush job. When I do move in...'

'Yes?' Oh, my God, he was going to ask her to move in with him. Her heart began to pound.

'I don't want you buying some cheap little place. Let me buy you something really nice.' His arms slid around her waist. 'It's the least I can do.'

She couldn't help the shudder of revulsion that swept through her. She closed her eyes, her thoughts weary. After all he's just said in his own defence he goes and makes a demeaning offer like that.

His voice held frustration. 'I see I've just made another boo-boo. Hell, I don't seem to be able to make the right moves where you're concerned, do I?' He startled her by wrenching away quite violently. 'What is it with you, anyway? What's wrong with a man looking after his woman, buying her a place to live in?'

'Nothing,' she said stiffly, 'if they're living together or married. But surely you can see any decent woman would be offended by such a suggestion? You make me sound like your paid mistress. You can't have your cake and eat it too, Aaron. You want to be free to come and go as you please. Then give me the same rights. I would hardly have them with you being my landlord! You'd expect me to be at your disposal, however and whenever you pleased. Forgive me if I say that sounds too close to prostitution for my liking. Or is that how you think of me, as little better than a prostitute?'

He threw up his hands, spun away from her and began to pace to and fro across the room. 'I don't believe this,' he ranted, his hands gesticulating wildly. 'I was so happy when I came over here. So happy. And now...'

He thumped the far end of the kitchen table. 'No, of course I don't damned well think of you as a prostitute! Far from it. God, I think you're a wonderful, beautiful, marvellous, spirited, strong, sexy woman.' He began walking towards her, his face softening to an expression of tender anguish. 'But still sweet...and fresh...and oddly old-fashioned in some ways. And I can't bear to think of my life without you in it.'

He stopped in front of her, his hands curling slowly over her shoulders. Serina was spellbound, both by his passionate outpouring and the warm, wondrous way his eyes were caressing hers. All she could do was stare up at him, aching for him to say what had to be in his heart, what had to be behind all these marvellous words: that he loved her.

But he didn't.

'I care about you,' he said instead. 'Very much...I admit I still don't want marriage or total commitment. That hasn't changed. But you're not that sort of person either, are you, Serina? If it were marriage and babies you were after you'd have taken that road long ago. I think you want what I want. The right to be an individual, to have one's own private space, but at the same time to have someone to be with, talk to; someone to hold, to touch, to kiss...'

His fingers dug into her shoulders as he lifted her mouth to his, and, while Serina was moved by his kiss, his last words had filled her with a dark dismay. He didn't have any idea what made her tick, what she wanted from life. He had interpreted her reluctance to settle for second best in a life partner over the years as a wish to be single and fancy-free.

But he was wrong, terribly wrong. Yet if she said all this their relationship would be over. All she could do was go along with what he wanted at the moment and keep hoping that eventually his aversion to marriage, or at least commitment, would lessen.

He drew back from the kiss at last, her willing response having smoothed the tension from his face. 'That's all settled, then?' he murmured, touching a gentle hand to her cheek. 'You'll at least let me help you *look* for a place, a unit near the beach perhaps?'

She plastered a smile on her face. Having made her decision, Serina was going to see it through to the bitter end. 'I'd like that.'

His sigh was full of relief. 'Thank God we got that all straightened out. For a moment there, I thought...' He shrugged, then bent to kiss her, deeply, hungrily.

Serina wished she could help the immediate and fierce response that sent a low moan to her throat. The kiss lasted for a long time, and when Aaron drew back he let her go to rub his chin, a rueful grimace on his lips. 'New Year's Eve, eh?'

'New Year's Eve,' she husked with true regret. But she could hardly say anything different now. Explanations would be far too awkward.

'Aah, well. *Out of Africa*, here we come...'

Serina was to think later how odd it was that, of all the films in the world, he'd had to choose one where the main love story revolved around a woman who wanted and needed the security of marriage, and an independent man who shied away from commitment. But it was indeed a wonderful movie, a thought-provoking and emotional one.

'I think,' she commented tearfully as the final credits came up, 'that if the hero hadn't been killed he would have married Karen.'

'I don't think so,' Aaron contradicted. 'He was too set in his ways. Anyway, there's no point in hypothesising—he *was* killed. It's a true story, not a Hollywood invention.'

'I guess you're right,' Serina murmured, not wanting to argue with him again. Besides, there was an edgy flavour to his voice that warned her to get off that subject.

'Would you like a cup of tea?' she asked.

They spent another couple of enjoyable hours just talking. Not on anything crucial. Mostly on various films they had seen, and enjoyed. Their tastes were surprisingly similar, neither of them liking the films that had little else to offer but gratuitous violence.

At last Aaron rose with a sigh. 'I have to go. I promised Christine I would take her out for a Chinese tonight. I'd ask you to come too but I think she's looking forward to having me all to herself for once.'

'Of course,' Serina smiled, and walked with him out to the car. 'Will I see you tomorrow?' she asked after he had kissed her goodbye.

He climbed in behind the wheel, wound down the window and smiled up at her. 'Silly question.'

Her heart turned over. 'When?'

'Sixish. How about dinner out and another movie?'

'Great. You're staying up here at Jillian's for a while, aren't you?'

'Till New Year's Eve. Then I'm going back to Sydney. Keep New Year's Eve free, will you?'

'Are we going to a party?' she said brightly.

His smile was wry. 'Not likely. Take *you* all glammed up into a room full of my boozy cronies?' He laughed. 'Heck, I'd have to spend all night keeping their paws and eyes off. The party I have in mind is definitely only for two!'

Serina tried to take his words in the joking manner they were delivered. But underneath she wished he would take her to a party, be openly proud and trusting of their relationship. Was he wary, perhaps, that he might flare up into a jealous rage if she so much as smiled at another man? Or did he just want to hide her away, solely for his eyes and pleasure? She wanted Aaron to love her, but not like that!

She took a step back and folded her arms, a shiver running up her spine. 'You can't be cold,' he frowned.

'Someone must have walked over my grave.'

The word 'grave' made his frown darken further, and Serina hastened to alleviate the situation. 'Off you go,' she urged. 'You don't want to worry Christine.'

He glanced at his watch. 'Yes, I'd better move it. See you,' he called as he fired the engine and sped off down the road.

Serina sighed when he turned the corner at the bottom of the hill. Why, oh, why, she wondered, couldn't she have fallen in love with a simple, uncomplicated man, a man who wanted exactly what she wanted? Marriage...security...a family...Instead, she had to get tangled up with Aaron. Did he love her yet? she asked herself for the umpteenth time. Or was it still mainly lust?

Could be, she admitted ruefully. Could be...

Serina turned and walked slowly into the house.

CHAPTER THIRTEEN

IT WAS the end of the first week in January and on that particular Saturday afternoon Aaron was going to help Serina fix up the lease for the unit she had decided to rent rather than buy. Aaron and Christine planned to move in to the house just as soon as Serina moved her personal things out.

At least that *had* been the plan.

But everything had changed now...

Serina sat at the kitchen table, her head in her hands, the reality of her situation finally sinking in. Her eyes began to swim, tears spilling out and down her cheeks, through her fingers. She could still hardly believe it.

Not that crying would do any good. Or solve anything. The die had been cast and nothing—absolutely *nothing*—could be done to change it!

Because, against all the odds, all the unlikely probabilities, she *was* pregnant.

She had gone to a twenty-four-hour medical centre early that morning because her still missing period had finally got the better of her. Not that she'd imagined for one moment she had conceived a child. Her mind had taken her along other, more traumatic routes. After all, she had taken all the necessary precautions and there had been no other symptoms to warn her. No morning sickness or dizziness. Not that there would be yet, she supposed in weary resignation.

Her first reaction to the doctor's diagnosis had been utter disbelief. But it was hard to ignore the test he had shown her, a test that was conclusive after a fort-night. From the dates she told him, the doctor had concluded that she had probably conceived the first time with Aaron, seventeen days before. On an internal examination he'd decided that the diaphragm she had been using was slightly too small for her and that, for some reason he couldn't pinpoint, her cycle must have been disturbed and ovulation delayed.

Had she been under any stress? he'd asked.

She had nodded dumbly.

An amazing and unfortunate set of circumstances, he'd replied, shaking his head.

She had left the surgery in a daze. A baby...she was going to have a baby...Aaron's baby...

And as much as she wanted the child—indeed would have their child no matter what!—Serina had realised immediately this spelt disaster for her and Aaron's relationship. *Disaster!*

For even if he did accept the child as his—and he might not!—he would naturally think she had deliberately got pregnant in order to trap him into marriage. Hadn't she taken responsibility for contraception? Didn't he believe she had recently had a period?

Possibly he might believe her if she told him the truth and got him to speak to the doctor, but either way this pregnancy spelt the end of their future together. He would hate the feeling of entrapment, hate the unwanted responsibility. He was sure to end up hating *her*!

By the time she had arrived home Serina was in a terrible state, her mind whirling. Maybe she was wrong. Maybe Aaron would take it quite well. Maybe he would confess that he loved her and wanted to marry her anyway. She was tempted. What woman wouldn't be? She loved the man and could hardly bear to think of life without him.

But, as the time of Aaron's arrival approached, Serina finally embraced the fact that she couldn't in all conscience tell him about the baby. Neither could she stay and live down here, with her pregnancy gradually becoming more obvious. Naomi had used such a tactic to ensnare Aaron, with awful results. Serina loved Aaron too much to subject him to such a ghastly replay of the past.

Her packing had been achieved with numbed movements, after which she made the necessary phone calls then sat down on the steps near the front door, elbows on knees, head in hands. Accept it, Serina, she told herself. It's over...

Strangely enough, she didn't feel like crying any more. She felt almost calm, resigned. At least she *was*, till Aaron arrived. Nerves crowded back when he breezed in, all smiles, and immediately swooped up her two bags. 'Glad to see you're ready, sweets,' he said, and started heading for the front door.

It was time, she realised, to tell him she had changed her mind, that she didn't want to live down here and be his lover, that she wanted to go back to Queensland to live by herself. She meant to tell him kindly, carefully, but nerves made the words tumble out of her mouth without preamble, without any possibility of softening their content.

Aaron just stared at her, his eyes rounding, his expression appalled.

She hated seeing the shock, the hurt on his face, but, having said it, she realised there was no easy way to say something like this, to *do* something like this. Maybe at some time in the future she would contact him and tell him about the baby, and maybe then he would be more ready to handle the news. As it was, she just knew it would make him unbelievably miserable.

Finally he dropped her bags, turning away only briefly to fling the front door shut before whirling to face her again. 'I don't believe what I just heard, Serina! Not a word of it! Something's happened I don't know about. What is it?' he demanded. 'Is it that stupid damned letter you got from that old boy-friend of yours? Paul something or other? Don't look so shocked. I didn't read it. I merely picked up the envelope and saw the name on the back.'

She looked up at him, fighting inside for the courage to go through with this. 'No, Paul doesn't want me back. He was just writing to let me know he'd found someone to marry at last and wished me well.'

'I see,' he scorned. 'So I'm not the first poor bastard you've screwed up. You've probably been loving and leaving 'em for years! My God,' he exclaimed, horror dawning in his eyes, 'don't tell you've met someone else?'

'No, of course not!' she denied hotly.

'What is it, then?' His eyes raked her face. 'Tell me, Serina, for pity's sake!'

'I can't,' she whispered.

'Can't, Serina?' he said harshly. 'Or won't? Hell, you can't expect me to let you walk out without some sort of an explanation. I deserve that at least, don't I?'

She could see he was determined for her to say something, give some reason, no matter how pathetic. 'It . . . it's not one single reason,' she began hesitantly. 'It's me, for one. I . . . I've never been able to settle down in one place for long. I get . . . restless. And then I move on. I really like you, Aaron. Very much. And

I thought I wanted a long-term relationship but I . . . I'm beginning to feel . . . smothered.'

He stared at her. 'Smothered?' he said, disbelief in his voice and eyes. Clearly, he wasn't convinced.

'Yes . . . You're a very jealous and possessive man, Aaron,' she went on. 'I can't handle that sort of thing. First there was that incident with Craig . . . and then there was the New Year's Eve party.'

'New Year's Eve party? Goddammit, we didn't even *go* to a New Year's Eve party!'

She flushed under his frustration. 'I know! That's just the point. And why didn't we? I'll tell you why. You didn't want any other man *looking* at me, let alone wanting me.'

She could see he was beginning to believe her, for there was an element of truth in what she was saying. 'And what will happen when you go back to work and we don't spend as much time together? I'll be getting the third degree all the time. It'll be a nightmare!'

She looked away from the shock in his face, fearing that at any moment she would throw herself in his arms and tell him the truth and to hell with it!

'I see,' he muttered. 'I didn't realise I was as bad as that. In fact I . . .' He broke off and just stared at her, long and hard, as though by searching her face he could see into her mind. Finally, a hard glint came into his gaze. 'I suppose there's nothing I can do to change your mind,' he bit out. 'Nothing I can say, no reassurances I can make?'

'No . . .'

'Look at me, damn you, when you say that!'

She lifted her lashes, unable to prevent the shimmering of tears in her eyes.

He saw them and shook his head, his expression anguished. 'Do you have any idea what you're doing to me?' he rasped. 'Any idea at all?'

'Yes.'

'I should wish you to hell.'

She just looked at him, knowing they were both already there.

He took a ragged step towards her, one hand reaching out to touch her cheek, to move across and trace the curve of her lips.

'Don't,' she cried, pushing away his hand to cradle her cheeks with her own hands. 'Please don't...'

There was an elongated silence.

'Are you leaving today?' he finally asked, his voice flat and empty.

She nodded.

'Do you want me to drive you anywhere?'

She shook her head.

'What about the unit? Have you rung the estate agent, told them you wouldn't be signing the lease?'

'Yes,' she choked out, looking up at last. 'And I quit my job.'

'That's it, then, isn't it? I suppose you'll want me to say your goodbyes to Jillian. And Christine.'

'If you would,' she said tensely.

His indifferent shrug betrayed more pain than the most callous words would have. 'Why not? What about the house keys?'

'I left them on the kitchen table.'

'How very organised you are, Serina.'

She accepted his sarcasm with a sad little smile. Not organised enough, it seemed, to prevent a pregnancy that was tearing her life to pieces. 'Goodbye, Aaron.'

'Don't mind me if I don't come out and see you off.' He glared at her one last time, then turned away and stalked into the house.

Serina would never know how she made it down to Rupert's home that day. She had secured her two bags on the back of her bike and taken off, wheels wobbling, tears streaming down her face, uncaring if she lived or died.

The ride was an endless road of misery and recriminations. She had handled the situation all wrong. She should have told Aaron the truth, should have done anything but let him look at her as he had done, with such hatred. She could bear almost anything but that!

She got lost several times, having to ask directions. But in the end she made it to Rupert's luxurious villa house, which was tucked away in a private leafy street in suburban Sans Souci. It was faintly Mediterranean in style, with archways, white-painted bricks and lots of plants.

He was watching the races on television when she arrived—his wife away at the hairdresser's in preparation for their first Saturday night at the theatre since coming back from their cruise. He settled back down on his deeply cushioned lounger after waving Serina impatiently inside and into an adjoining chair. But when she announced her news her jerked forward to sit on the edge of the seat, snapping off the TV with the remote control.

'You're *what*?' he exploded.

'I said I'm pregnant with Aaron Kingsley's child.'

For a split second Rupert merely stared up at her, his penetrating blue eyes quite blank. But then his brain clicked into gear and he sighed back into the cushions. 'Well, well, well! I would have thought you'd have known better than that, Sister·dear. You've avoided such an occurrence quite successfully for long enough.' His eyes narrowed with an unexpected idea. 'Or was it deliberate?'

'No... a fluke.'

'So why are you telling me? Surely you don't expect me to play big brother after all these years? You've always made it perfectly clear you despised both Philip and myself almost as much as you despised Father.'

She gaped at him.

His face showed genuine surprise. 'You *didn't* despise us all?'

'Of course not. Never! I... I thought it was the other way round. You and Philip were always so superior, so... *sneering*. And as for Dad, he never had any time for me. He thought I was nothing but a little... a little...'

'Slut?' Rupert suggested bluntly.

'Maybe not as bad as that...'

'Dad adored you,' Rupert announced baldly. 'Maybe even more than Mum did.'

'But he... he...'

Rupert sighed. 'You were his little princess, Serina. His sweet, innocent little princess. Then suddenly you grew up. *Very* suddenly. He couldn't handle it, couldn't handle the way all the boys—and men— started looking at you. He didn't know what to do so he got angry, then blamed you, drove you away. It was easier than feeling impotent about the situation.'

'I never knew... never realised...'

'You know, Serina, for a woman of the world you're surprisingly innocent. But that's perhaps what gets the males in where you're concerned. That stunning sensuality of yours is tinged with a maddening innocence. It used to drive Phil mad the way all his classmates suddenly began flocking around the house once you started blossoming, all just to see you, of course. Poor Phil, he always did have trouble making friends, especially girlfriends. That's why he ate so much, and why he was always so aggressively rude to you, because he was jealous of the way you attracted the opposite sex like flies.'

Serina shook her head. 'I feel so stupid not knowing any of this.'

'Not to worry. Phil survived and Evonne adores him. They're talking about a baby themselves next year.'

'Oh, I'm so glad.'

Rupert made an impatient sound. 'And that's just like you, too.'

'What do you mean?'

'You're genuinely happy for him, aren't you, even though he's treated you like dirt for years? Do you know how annoying it is to have someone so generous around? It makes one feel lousy. Next thing you know I'll be doing something stupid like giving you my share of the house-money for that kid you're having.'

Serina gaped at her brother.

'You don't have to look at me like that,' he protested in his best bored tone. 'Someone has to do something. I gather your precious Mr Kingsley isn't jumping up and down with joy at becoming a father, which is why you're here. Am I right?'

'Not quite,' she managed to get out. 'I couldn't think where else to go on the spur of the moment. Aaron doesn't know. And I'm *not* going to tell him.'

'Oh, dear God, why not?'

There was no way she could explain her decision without telling Rupert the whole truth. It took some time but to her surprise her elder brother listened with great tolerance, even supplying tissues and patting her shoulder when she dissolved into the occasional weep.

'Now let me get this straight,' he said when she'd finished. 'The real reason you're not telling your erstwhile lover of his impending fatherhood is that you think he couldn't handle such a crushing responsibility at this point in time but that he would embrace it nevertheless, all the while heading for a nervous breakdown.'

'Something like that,' she sniffed, thinking Rupert had described the situation in typically wordy legal-style jargon.

'So you lied and left him, basically because you love him.'

'Well . . . yes.'

'Brother, it sounds like a line from a soap opera!'

He shook his head in exasperation, but when her chin began to quiver dangerously his face melted to an expression that almost resembled affection. Serina was astonished. 'I guess it's up to your family to help you, then,' he sighed.

'If I could just stay a couple of nights,' she began hesitantly. 'I thought I would go back to Queensland and use my share of the estate to buy a small unit. They're cheaper up there than down here. Then I could get a job till the baby's due and——'

'Definitely not!'

'No?'

'Oh, you can go to Queensland if you like. I wouldn't presume to tell you where to live, but you shouldn't have to work in your condition. I meant what I said, you know, about giving you my share of the estate. I don't really need it anyway. That way you can buy a decent place with half and have enough left over to give you a small income.'

'But...but,' she flustered, 'I can't let you do that! I mean, I'm incredibly moved and grateful but it's not right. I won't accept it.'

'Typical,' Rupert sighed. 'You always were fiercely independent. How about an interest-free loan, payments starting after the babe is old enough for you to go back to work?'

'Rupert...' Tears were back in her eyes again. 'I don't know what to say...'

'Thank you will suffice,' he said, a catch in his normally cold voice.

'But what about your wife?' she whispered. 'Won't she object?'

'Not at all. She'll be delighted for there to be a baby in the family she can buy things for and spoil. You see, I can't have children...'

'Oh, Rupert... How awful for you...'

He cleared his throat. 'It's not so bad for me—I have my career, after all—but Vivian is beginning to feel it. I guess I over-compensate by buying her things.'

'But, Rupert, if there's nothing wrong with Vivian why doesn't she try artificial insemination?'

Her brother pulled a face. 'She mentioned it once but I don't think I could treat anyone else's kid as my own.'

'That's silly, and selfish... and you know it.'

He gave Serina a sharp glance. 'You've learnt to speak your mind, haven't you?'

Her smile was wry. 'Just like you.'

'*Touché.*'

They grinned at each other, and suddenly, despite her heartache over losing Aaron, everything didn't seem quite so black in Serina's world.

CHAPTER FOURTEEN

SERINA had been settled into her new unit for just on three months when Philip rang her one night in a flap. A phone call from him was not unusual—he often rang her now—but it was not like him to sound so rattled.

'I'm terribly sorry,' he said again. 'I didn't mean to tell him. I *know* you made Rupert and me promise not to under any circumstances but, my God, when that man gets mad he's positively frightening!'

'You told Aaron I was pregnant,' she stated flatly, her whole body going cold, then hot, then cold.

'Of course not! I wouldn't do that. It was your address he wanted.'

'And you *gave* it to him? Just because he got a bit angry? Oh, Philip, how *could* you?'

'Hey, you weren't here, so don't judge me too harshly. It wasn't just a question of anger. He threatened to put a private detective on your tail. He said he knew you'd intended buying a unit somewhere on the Gold Coast so it wouldn't have taken a decent investigator very long to locate you. A month at most. I thought if your Mr Kingsley was going to come up and see you it was best he did so as soon as possible, before you're too obviously pregnant. This way, at least you can hide it if you want to. But to be honest, Serina, why not tell the man, give him a chance?'

Serina's sigh was ragged. 'Believe me, Philip, he'd rather not know. Are you sure he's going to come up here to see me? What about my phone number? Did you give him that?'

'No, and since it's not listed under your name he'll have to go up there to see you personally or not at all. And he will. I'd stake my life on it. I've never seen a man so damned determined!'

'Oh, God...'

'I tried ringing you as soon as he left the office but you weren't home. I've been ringing every hour since. Where on earth were you?'

Serina just caught herself before she said 'At work'. Rupert and Philip had been so good to her, Rupert with his loan, and Philip stunning her by giving her a small car—a bike, he'd said, was hardly suitable transport for a woman in her condition—so she didn't like to confess that she didn't have enough to live on till her first interest cheque came in and had taken a casual job as a barmaid down at a small local hotel to tide her over.

'I was out all afternoon,' she said. 'Do you think Aaron's already on his way?'

'Maybe... Maybe not. He'd drive, I'd say. I'd certainly be keeping an eye out for him tomorrow.'

Serina's head spun. Tomorrow... She couldn't think... didn't know what to do...

She sank down on the chair that was next to the phone, her free hand coming to rest on the slight swell of her stomach, her emotions mixed. She could hide her pregnancy quite easily. But was she sure she wanted to any more? Time had given her many moments to regret her decision. She had missed Aaron so terribly...

'Serina? Are you OK?'

'What? Oh, yes, Philip, I'm fine.'

'You always say you're fine. I could fly up in the morning if you're worried, give you some moral support.'

'Thank you, dear brother, but I'll be all right. Truly.'

'Hmph! You just don't like admitting you need help. If you lived down here in Sydney Rupert and I could keep a better eye on you.'

But that would have been too temptingly near to Aaron, she almost said. Five hundred miles was a safe distance. At least it had been. Till now...

Why was Aaron coming to see her? It seemed unlikely he wanted her back. Serina had not forgotten how he had looked at her that final day, his face dark and unforgiving. And it had been over three months, after all. If he'd missed her so badly he would surely have come after her before this.

'Well, if you're not going to talk I might as well hang up,' Philip said peevishly.

'Sorry... I was a million miles away.'

'Well you'd better get your wits about you before lover-boy shows up. That man doesn't know how to take a simple "no" for an answer.'

They said their goodbyes, but even after the receiver was safely back in its cradle Serina just sat there, staring into space, her mind going round and round. Why was he coming? Why?

In the end she jumped to her feet and vacuumed the whole place, more to do something than with any desire to clean up. She kept thinking of coming home after work and seeing his blue BMW parked in the street outside the block of units, waiting for her.

Serina didn't sleep well that night, if at all. She contemplated ringing the hotel in the morning and saying she wouldn't be in to work, but that would have been risking her job, which she needed. So ten a.m. found her behind the main bar as usual, serving their first batch of customers.

'Haven't seen you in here before, darlin',' the truckie lounging on the counter drawled. He lifted the schooner of beer to his lips while his insolent gaze roved over her figure. Not that it was on display. She had left her white shirt out to flow over the tightening waistband of her black skirt.

'I've been here three months.' She shrugged and began drying glasses. A yawn came to her mouth.

'Late to bed?' the man suggested.

'Something like that.'

He gave a knowing laugh. 'You should try going alone.'

She raised a dry eyebrow at him. Men who liked to talk about sex were rarely a problem.

'You could be a model, you know,' he continued.

'Is that so?'

'I'd like to take pictures of you.'

'Really.'

'Yeah . . . I'm good with a camera. I'm good with other things, too . . .' His eyes dropped down to her breasts then up again. 'What do you say, eh? When do you finish up here?'

Serina rolled her eyes and turned away.

'Aw, come on, honey. I haven't got time for games.'

'Too bad,' came a low, menacing voice. 'I was just about to give you your first lesson in survival training.'

Both the truckie's and Serina's heads snapped round.

'Aaron . . .' Serina lowered the glass to the counter, her hand shaking slightly, her heart going thumpity-thump.

'Serina,' he said, nodding towards her.

God, he looked like hell. Unshaven. Bleary-eyed. Crumpled clothes.

But at the same time he looked magnificent, with his squared shoulders and steely gaze striking terror into the heart of the little creep at the bar.

'No need to get steamed, mate,' the truckie was blustering. 'I was only talkin' to her. No harm done.'

'Shove off, buddie,' Aaron growled. *'Fast!'*

'Sure thing, mate. Sure thing.' And he scuttled out without finishing his beer.

Aaron slid on to the bar stool, his eyes lifting to Serina's. A reluctant smile came to his lips. 'Things haven't changed around you, I see.'

Against all the best dictates of common sense she smiled back at him. 'Oh, I don't know,' she murmured with hidden irony. 'Can I get you a beer?' She swept aside the half-empty schooner.

'Why not?'

'What about food? Are you hungry? You look hungry.'

That slow smile tugged again at his mouth. 'Oh, yes...I'm hungry...'

'I'll get Rex to make you a couple of sandwiches. It's too early for a proper lunch. The cook hasn't arrived yet.' She moved off to speak to the hotel proprietor, who gave Aaron a close look before nodding and heading for the kitchen.

Serina appeared totally composed as she walked slowly back, stopping to pull a beer for Aaron on the way. 'Here it comes.' She slid it along the counter to a perfect halt in front of him, hoping this would distract him from looking too closely at her figure as she walked back.

'Very professional,' he drawled, and lifted it to his lips.

'I've had plenty of practice.'

He sipped the beer, then put it down. 'You don't seem all that surprised by my arrival. I suppose Philip rang you, warned you.'

'Yes.'

'I went to your place first. A neighbour told me where you worked.'

'You must have just missed me. I started at ten.'

He nodded. 'Can we talk? Here? Now? It's important to me, Serina.'

Despite Aaron's surface calm, his voice had vibrated with a tension that was disturbing. Her chest contracted, making her aware of how tightly she was holding on to herself to appear at ease.

'I suppose so. We're not busy yet. I'll just speak to Rex and get your sandwiches.'

'I'll be over in that booth in the corner.'

For a second Serina hesitated, worried that he might notice the change in her figure as she walked across the hotel floor. But she needn't have worried. Aaron didn't even look up from staring into the beer till she slid into the booth opposite and put the sandwiches in front of him.

'You're looking well,' he murmured, his eyes unreadable as they met hers.

'Sorry if I can't say the same for you,' she countered. 'You look like hell.'

'Driving all night does take it out of one.'

'So why do it, Aaron? What was the awful rush? Did you have to meet one of your deadlines?'

His smile was wry. 'Same old Serina . . . as blunt as ever.'

'Not blunt, Aaron. Just straightforward. Now are you going to tell me why you've driven all this way in such a hurry? It's not Christine, is it?' she said, her stomach turning over with the sudden thought. 'She's not sick or anything?'

His laugh was definitely sardonic. 'No.'

Serina sighed.

'I wonder if I would rate the same concern. What would you say if *I* was sick?'

Her heart stopped. 'You're not, are you?'

'Yes.'

All the colour drained from her face.

His hands shot across the table to grasp hers, his expression twisting into an anguished grimace. 'Sick with missing you, Serina. Sick with waking up and not finding you next to me. Sick with looking in the mirror and thinking that I drove you away.'

'Aaron . . . please . . .' She could hardly believe what she was hearing, dared not believe the awesome depth of emotion that was vibrating in his voice.

'I love you, Serina,' he rasped.

Her head rocked backwards, all breathing suspended. 'You . . . love me?'

'Desperately. And you can say what you like, make any excuse you like, but I *know* you loved me once.'

She blinked her astonishment. 'How . . . how do you know?'

'I think I always did know. That's why I was so stunned by your leaving me. It just didn't make sense. It didn't make sense to Craig either.'

'Craig?' she gasped.

'Yes, Craig. He kept telling me there had to be some mistake, he was so sure you loved me.' He lifted her hands to his mouth, kissing her fingers. 'You *did*, didn't you?'

Her head nodded before she could stop it.

His relief was enormous, though she could guess what question he was going to ask next. 'Then why did you leave, Serina? I don't believe you were restless, or that I was excessively jealous. We were happy together. I know we were! Could it have been because you thought you had no future with me, because I refused to even consider marriage and a family?'

Her eyes opened wide, her lips parting with a small gasp.

'You don't have to say anything,' he went on swiftly, his face showing even more relief. 'I can see it in your face. Oh, Serina...darling... What a fool I've been...'

All she could do was blink.

'After you'd gone I almost went mad,' he went on passionately. 'I had no idea how much, how deeply I loved you till you weren't there. It wasn't just the sex, either. I missed hearing you laugh, seeing you smile, watching you do even the simplest things. I even missed your sarcasm. I couldn't believe how blind I had been, thinking that, because of what I'd been through with Naomi, I didn't want love or commitment any more. Without it—without *you*—I was like an empty shell.'

He was shaking his head. 'Dear God, Serina, life isn't worth living unless one needs and is needed in return. I suddenly realised that more than anything else in the world I wanted you as my wife, to have a child by you, because I knew that with you it would be a real partnership, a sharing. Not one person taking and the other giving. You are everything I want and need, my darling. Everything!'

He pressed both her palms to his mouth, kissing them hungrily. 'Say you still love me!' he demanded in a thick strangled voice. 'Say you'll marry me! Say you want my child!'

Her eyes swam as she pulled his hands across the small table to *her* mouth. There she kissed them reverently then held them against her cheek till she could catch her breath. 'I still love you, Aaron... I want to marry you... But I...'

He flinched when she hesitated, his face grimacing with apprehension.

'I'm already having your child,' she murmured.

He wrenched his hands away and sagged back against the booth, clearly staggered. 'My God...' But as he stared at her astonishment gradually changed to confusion. As though in slow motion he came forward to lean against the table. 'But...but...how? When?'

'The first night we slept together, I think.'

'But you said... and later you...'

Serina's smile was gentle, her heart overflowing, for, while Aaron was puzzled, there was no disbelief in his face, no rush to accuse, of condemn. 'I think I'd better start at the beginning.'

So she told him everything, not just from the beginning of their relationship but everything that had shaped her life from the moment she had begun to grow into a woman. She told him what had led up to her leaving home, about her long lonely years living in Queensland, and finally about Paul. Aaron was clearly taken aback when she revealed she'd been a virgin before that, but he accepted it without question, then showed a heart-warming satisfaction when she added that he, Aaron, had been the only man she had ever loved, the only man who had made her sexually happy. The only reason she had never confessed her relative inexperience earlier was because it had seemed to please him that she was a free spirit.

Last but not least, she related the extraordinary chain of circumstances surrounding the conception of their child.

And with the telling she saw Aaron's love for her grow and flower as true love did with the emergence of trust and understanding. He looked at her with new eyes, new respect. And a large degree of awe.

'Do you mean to tell me that you left because you thought I couldn't cope with our having a baby, that you were prepared to sacrifice your own happiness for mine?'

She shrugged, feeling shy under his adoring gaze. 'It seemed the right thing to do. Craig insisted you weren't ready yet to take on any more responsibility. I thought that I might tell you . . . some time in the future . . .'

'Craig . . .' Aaron breathed in and out very deeply. 'I'll kill him!'

'But he was right, Aaron,' she insisted. 'You wouldn't have been able to handle it three months ago. At least now, having loved and lost, so to speak, you know what you really want out of life.'

'True,' he nodded, then shook his head regretfully. 'But when I think of what you've gone through—I should have been there for you, looking after you, loving you. Oh, Serina . . . Can you ever forgive me?'

'How can I forgive you for something you didn't know, Aaron? It's I who should be asking your forgiveness. I hurt you too with my lies, though I certainly didn't mean or want to. I thought it was a case of being cruel to be kind.'

He simply stared at her. 'I've never known a woman like you. You are truly remarkable.'

'I'm no saint, Aaron,' she denied. 'I've had some terrible nights, missing you, wanting you. Many times I hated the decision I made. In fact, I'm not too sure I wouldn't have relented soon and told you. It was too lonely without you.'

He reached forward and enfolded her hands back within his. 'You'll never be lonely again, my darling. Never...'

Her heart filled to overflowing, tears pricking her eyes. Fairy-tales did come true. Or was it more perhaps that love had won through in the end, her love for this man of her dreams?

The emotion of the moment was diffused when Aaron's mouth broke into a cheeky grin. 'At least once I take you home with me and announce our coming marriage I'll be welcomed back into the family fold. Jillian isn't talking to me.'

'Goodness. What happened?' Serina was all ears, glad to put any tears aside. This wasn't a time for crying. This was a joyous, a wondrous moment.

Aaron gave a mock shudder. 'After you left, whenever I visited it was like being dipped in the Antarctic. Poor Gerald tried to be a mediator but failed miserably. Finally, last week, I blew my stack and demanded to know what was eating her, whereupon Jillian pronounced I was a rotten cad who didn't deserve the love of a good woman, and that if I didn't find you and marry you she wouldn't speak to me for the rest of her life. Of course, I told her to mind her own bloody business and charged off home. My infernal male ego had convinced me you were nothing but an empty, flighty bit of fluff who'd never be able to be relied on and who wasn't worth chasing after.'

His laughter hid a lot of remembered pain. 'God, the rubbish I told myself! Then two nights ago they replayed *Out of Africa* on TV. I vowed I wouldn't watch it, wouldn't do anything to remind myself of you, but Christine insisted on seeing it and soon I was sitting there, watching the hero get killed again. It came to me that I could die tomorrow without telling you that I loved you, without ever holding you in my arms again. I resolved then and there that I could not let that happen. So I went to see your brother, and here I am!'

'Oh, Aaron...'

He just looked at her, a soft smile of wonder on his lips. 'A baby,' he murmured. 'Our baby...' His smile grew. 'You do realise Christine is going to flip. She always wanted a brother or a sister.'

'A brother,' she informed him. 'I've had an ultrasound.'

His eyes lit up. 'A son...'

Her gaze searched his for one last reassurance. 'Are you positive it's all right, Aaron? I mean...you might have wanted a baby eventually, but——'

He put a finger to her lips. 'None of that. I'm delighted and ecstatic. And I don't think of your pregnancy as a fluke, as you said. It's as though from the moment we met your body waited for me, waited for me to bring it to life in the most marvellous way...'

'Oh, darling...I never thought of it like that. Oh...' Her eyes did fill with tears this time. 'What a lovely way to look at it...'

'Hey! Serina! That's a bloke's not hassling you, is he?' Rex called from the bar.

She looked up and smiled through her soggy lashes. 'This bloke, Rex, is the father of my baby and my husband-to-be. And no, he's not hassling me.'

'Baby? Husband?' The hotel proprietor groaned. 'Oh, no, don't tell me. You're quitting!'

Aaron slid out from the booth and helped Serina to her feet. For a brief moment he stared in awe at her softly swelling stomach before curling an arm round her shoulders. ''Fraid so, mate,' Aaron called back. 'As of now!'

'Hey, but . . .'

Aaron drew out his wallet and threw two-hundred dollars on the bar-top. 'Drinks are on me,' he said.

Then he steered his lovely Serina out of the hotel and into the sunshine, where he stopped to look up into the clear blue sky.

'Great day for the race, isn't it?'

Serina frowned. 'The race? What race?'

He grinned. 'The human race.'

'Oh, *you*!'

They laughed and walked off, arm in arm, the love on their faces a tangible thing for all to bear witness to. It could be seen on the day of their wedding, and at the christening of their son a few months later.

Not a day went by when Serina did not thank the lord above for Aaron and his love.

And as for Aaron . . . whenever he looked at his breathtakingly beautiful wife his heart would literally turn over, and he would recall what Craig had once told him so succinctly. 'You're a lucky devil, mate. A very lucky devil!'

Share the adventure—and the romance—of

HARLEQUIN PRESENTS®

A Year DOWN UNDER

If you missed any titles in this miniseries,
here's your chance to order them:

Harlequin Presents®—A Year Down Under

#11519	HEART OF THE OUTBACK by Emma Darcy	$2.89	❏
#11527	NO GENTLE SEDUCTION by Helen Bianchin	$2.89	❏
#11537	THE GOLDEN MASK by Robyn Donald	$2.89	❏
#11546	A DANGEROUS LOVER by Lindsay Armstrong	$2.89	❏
#11554	SECRET ADMIRER by Susan Napier	$2.89	❏
#11562	OUTBACK MAN by Miranda Lee	$2.99	❏
#11570	NO RISKS, NO PRIZES by Emma Darcy	$2.99	❏
#11577	THE STONE PRINCESS by Robyn Donald	$2.99	❏
#11586	AND THEN CAME MORNING by Daphne Clair	$2.99	❏
#11595	WINTER OF DREAMS by Susan Napier	$2.99	❏
#11601	RELUCTANT CAPTIVE by Helen Bianchin	$2.99	❏
#11611	SUCH DARK MAGIC by Robyn Donald	$2.99	❏

(limited quantities available on certain titles)

TOTAL AMOUNT	$
POSTAGE & HANDLING	$
($1.00 for one book, 50¢ for each additional)	
APPLICABLE TAXES*	$ _____
TOTAL PAYABLE	$ _____
(check or money order—please do not send cash)	

To order, complete this form and send it, along with a check or money order for the total above, payable to Harlequin Books, to: *In the U.S.*: 3010 Walden Avenue, P.O. Box 9047, Buffalo, NY 14269-9047; *In Canada*: P.O. Box 613, Fort Erie, Ontario, L2A 5X3.

Name: _____

Address: _____ City: _____

State/Prov.: _____ Zip/Postal Code: _____

*New York residents remit applicable sales taxes.
Canadian residents remit applicable GST and provincial taxes.   YDUF

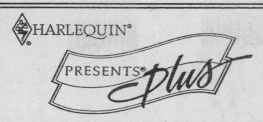

POSTCARDS FROM EUROPE

HARLEQUIN PRESENTS®

Hi!
Spending a year in Europe. You won't believe how great the men are! Will be visiting Greece, Italy, France and more.
Wish you were here—how about joining us in January?

There's a handsome Greek just waiting to meet you.

THE ALPHA MAN
by Kay Thorpe

Harlequin Presents #1619

Available in January wherever Harlequin books are sold.

HPPFEG